THE OTHER
DANIEL

A GRISHAM & SULLIVAN SHORT SUSPENSE THRILLER

JOHN HARDY BELL

SECOND
SIGHT
PUBLISHING

This is a work of fiction. All of the organizations, characters, and events portrayed in this novel are either products of the author's imagination or are used fictitiously.

For more, visit www.johnhardybell.com

For Jackie. My light. My love.

Between 2008 and 2012, Daniel Alexander Sykes savagely murdered twenty-seven people, including the FBI agent who was attempting to capture him. Sykes was a monster in every sense of the word – a true representation of the worst that humanity had to offer. And as the grisly details of his four-year crime spree slowly emerged, no sane person would have dared argued otherwise.

But as you are about to read, there is much more to Daniel Sykes than the man who the world came to know as 'The Circle Killer'. He was a first-grade teacher from Kutztown, Pennsylvania, a loving husband, a doting father, and, dare it be said, a human being. By the time you are finished with this book, you may very well want to label me more pathologically twisted than the subject I am writing about. Or you may come to a more rational and balanced conclusion: that it is very easy to judge someone without first knowing everything about them. But it isn't always fair to do so.

~Excerpt from Jacob Deaver's *THE OTHER DANIEL*

PROLOGUE

A CHANGE IN PLANS

Meredith Park slowly exhaled as she put the two-paragraph manuscript down on her desk, only now realizing that she had been holding her breath the entire time she was reading it.

The author of the manuscript sat across from her, nervous anticipation accentuating the tightness of his face. "So? What do you think?"

Meredith carefully considered her reply as she scanned the top of the page. "I think the title is brilliant."

The author smiled the same way all authors smiled when they heard the 'B' word. Images of Hemmingway and Salinger were undoubtedly swirling through his head, and Meredith knew she had to bring him back into the realm of the living - quickly.

"But I'm not seeing much else of value here."

She had never seen a face drop faster.

"I'm sorry, Jacob. I've always believed in the concept, and I still do. But the fact of the matter is that it's been three months since you've collected your advance. I know I don't have to preach to you about the importance of deadlines and given your track record I'm confident you'll find a way to meet this one. I just thought there would be a little more meat on the bone by now."

Jacob Deaver's stiff posture was betrayed by the pronounced quivering of his chin. It was a reaction that Meredith had seen too many times before. In her experience, writers were the most prideful human beings on the planet, and no matter how much they extolled the virtues of honest feedback, deep down the only feedback they truly valued was the kind that confirmed the perfection of their words. Entering her tenth year as a literary agent, Meredith had come across perfection only a handful of times. In three years of critiquing his work, Jacob had yet to come close. But *The Other Daniel* contained all the necessary elements of a potential bestseller: dark subject matter, intriguing players, and most importantly, controversy. It was the kind of book that got people talking. And no matter if that talk was positive or negative, it was still talk, which in Meredith's business was everything. She was on the verge of reminding her client of this potential but felt no need to further inflate his ego. She needed words on the page. And no matter how much potential the book had, two paragraphs in three months simply wasn't enough.

"The publisher hasn't asked for a progress report yet, but it's only a matter of time. And when the time does come, they are going to expect a lot more than this. Frankly I expect more too. A lot of people are sticking their necks out to get this to press. It's time to give them a reason to believe that it's worth it." She sighed, then slid the manuscript in his direction. "What are you going to do to make them believe?"

Jacob eyed the page as if the answer was hidden somewhere deep in the margins. "It's going to come together, Meredith." His tired brown eyes communicated a doubt that his words did not.

"How? When?"

"The outline is finished, and the basic narrative is laid out. The problem has been getting people to talk to me."

5

"I thought all you needed was some background on the guy. How hard is it to get people to talk about what kind of teacher he was?"

"Now that word is spreading that this book is some kind of sympathy piece on Sykes, which we both know isn't true, it's been incredibly hard. I've been to Pennsylvania twice now. I've seen where Sykes grew up, visited the school he taught in, I even sat through a church service with his old pastor. The people I encountered couldn't have been nicer, until I told them who I was and what I was doing there. Then *I* suddenly felt like the mass-murderer. People hate this man. Even the ones who love him hate him. To them, the life he lived prior to becoming a killer doesn't even exist."

For the duration of Jacob's ham-handed explanation, Meredith found herself doodling on her desktop calendar. It was a portrait of her family - husband, herself, and three daughters in stick figure form with tall grass, lush trees, and a smiling sun high above. Her six-year-old would have been proud of the craftsmanship. The doodle was designed to keep her calm, to maintain perspective, to prevent her from unleashing an unruly temper on her already fragile client. It only worked for a moment.

"Correct me if I'm wrong, but I assumed the purpose of this book was to use the people in Sykes' life – namely family and friends - to show the world that he was more than the headlines portrayed him to be."

Jacob ran fingers across the dense stubble on his otherwise smooth, youthful face. "That's right."

"So if you can't talk to these people, you don't have a book. Is that what you're telling me?"

The author's long frame sank deep into his chair, weighed down by the defeat of her perceived rejection. In addition to being prideful, writers were entirely too damn sensitive, Meredith thought. She forced a smile in hopes of easing the tension.

"Okay, what do you say we change course here and do a little brainstorming. Is there anyone on your list whom you haven't yet spoken to?"

Jacob remained quiet and Meredith could see the wheels of his memory turning. When his blank eyes met hers a few moments later, she knew what the outcome of his mental query had been. Still, she waited for him to say it.

"Not really."

Meredith's sigh was louder than she intended.

"Cut me some slack here, would you? It's not like I can talk to any of Sykes' victims. In case you haven't kept up with the story, they're all dead. That leaves me with a bunch of family members and friends who spend most of their waking hours trying to disown the guy. I've tried just about everything short of putting a gun to their heads. Trust me, no one is biting."

The resolve in Jacob's voice almost had Meredith convinced of the futility of the project and she had just begun contemplating how she was going to recoup the publisher's advance. Then she thought about something Jacob said: *I've tried just about everything short of putting a gun to their heads.* It came to her like a flash of light, so brilliant that it almost blinded her. An idea. A solution. A book.

"Camille Grisham."

Jacob's mouth flew open before he could formulate the words to come out of it. "The FBI agent?"

"Former FBI agent," Meredith corrected. "Look, I understand it's a bit outside of the box."

"A bit?"

"But it's also the perfect angle. Camille is the only person we know of who saw the worst of Sykes and lived to tell the tale."

"The problem is she isn't telling that tale to anyone. Do you know how many people have angled for the rights to her story? We're talking huge names offering huge money. And Camille has said no each and every time. What makes you think she'd give me two seconds, let alone enough sit-down material for an entire book?"

He made a good point, and deep-down Meredith knew he was probably right. But she refused to let her enthusiasm be sobered by something as trivial as reality. She wrote the words 'tortured FBI agent equals guaranteed bestseller' next to her family doodle, and knew that in the world she operated in, it absolutely did. The look of borderline horror that colored Jacob's face let her know just how far in she would have to dig her heels in order to convince him. Fortunately for Meredith, nobody dug deeper.

"If we can assure the publisher that this is possible, *The Other Daniel* immediately becomes their top priority. That means a faster pub date, comprehensive marketing, and an author whose value suddenly becomes immeasurable."

The expression on Jacob's face softened as the wheels in his mind started turning again. Meredith knew exactly which buttons to push and how hard to push them. In Jacob's case, the celebrity-author button worked every time.

"Granted it will be tough getting to her," she continued. "But if you do, if *The Other Daniel* hits shelves with Camille Grisham front and center, you can spend the rest of your career writing your own ticket. Doesn't that make the effort worthwhile?"

Without saying a word, Jacob pulled out his cell phone. He punched the keypad for several minutes before Meredith finally decided he wasn't going to let her in on his query.

"May I ask?" she said, offended by his absence of consideration.

"You know her best friend was murdered two days after she left the FBI, right?" he said without looking up from the phone.

Meredith's eyes dropped to the Pilot pen that she had been twirling in her hand. "I'm aware of that."

Jacob continued scrolling. "Then you're also aware of the crazy claim she's making about who is involved."

"According to some people, the claim isn't so crazy. Still, it sounds like she's going to have a hard time proving it, no matter how determined she is to do so."

"Knowing all of that, do you honestly think I'd have an iota of a chance with her? Daniel Sykes is something of a sore subject to begin with. I don't think she's going to appreciate someone showing up at her doorstep attempting to reopen that wound when she's still dealing with a fresh one."

"Like I said, Camille is determined to tell her story. The problem is no one is hearing that story. You have the opportunity to give her a voice."

Jacob smirked. "I'm a regular patron saint."

"I'm being serious. Make her believe that she's getting just as much out of this as you are and you won't have any problem getting her to open up."

"How exactly does talking about Daniel Sykes benefit her current situation?"

"You write your sympathy piece, only instead of focusing on Sykes, focus on Camille. The world deserves to know what really happened during that confrontation, and what happened to her as a result. Get people to understand Camille's back story and they might be more apt to listen to her regarding her friend's murder. Win for her, win for you. Actually, Pulitzer Prize for you." The gleam in Meredith's soft brown eyes was trumped by the wide smile that had spread across her angular face. She was pushing all the right buttons again.

With a gleam of his own, Jacob returned to his phone - same silent scrolling routine as before.

"What are you looking at now?" Meredith asked, feeling slighted for a second time.

"The next flight to Denver."

Suddenly she didn't feel the least bit slighted. "So, Camille is our girl?"

Jacob tucked his phone into his pocket as he stood up. The white Oxford shirt he wore was wrinkled and at least two sizes too big. Meredith made a note to recommend a stylist befitting the world's next great true-crime author. And if she had anything to say about it, that is exactly what Jacob Deaver was going to be.

"Camille is our girl," he said with confidence.

"The only problem is that she hasn't been seen much in public lately. How will you even know where to find her?"

"Promise me that Pulitzer and I'll go to the ends of the earth if I have to."

For the sake of their bestseller, Meredith hoped like hell that he meant it.

CHAPTER ONE

THE SHARK

The City Perk Café was a trendy little coffee shop located in a section of the city that felt overrun with trendy little coffee shops. Like most of the others, it was normally crowded with wide-eyed college students pounding away at their Apple MacBooks and sipping delicately on their custom-made cappuccinos. If you weren't one of them, the air of determined self-importance created by their collective efforts could be suffocating. As a result, Camille Grisham rarely allowed herself to stay longer than the five minutes it took to make her no-whip skinny mocha.

On this particular morning, however, the City Perk was nearly empty – a first in the two months that she had been coming here. Without the hordes of twenty-something's occupying every square inch of space the atmosphere was bright, like one of those festive French bistros you see on the Travel Channel. Having not spent much time in bright atmospheres lately, she couldn't resist the opportunity to take a seat while she waited for her coffee.

"If you want to hang out, I'd be happy to put this in a mug for you," the barista whose name Camille couldn't remember said when she noticed her sitting.

With little on her agenda other than the fruitless hours she planned to spend staring at a blank notebook with the words PRO and CON written at the top, Camille decided to grab a newspaper, stake out a small table in the back, and take in as much of this Travel Channel experience as she could. "A mug would be great," she told the barista with a smile that wasn't entirely manufactured.

For more than an hour she skimmed the morning paper, sipped delicately at her latte the way the college kids did, and allowed herself to simply exist. Normal, just like everyone else. There had been moments of normal in the past six months, but they were always fleeting, like the illusion of liquid blue in an otherwise barren desert. Even though Camille worried that this moment of normal would eventually meet the same fate, she basked in it nonetheless.

Only a handful of customers entered the café during her time there. A few took up seats in the empty tables around her, huddled in close conversation or staring intently at their electronic tablets. The rest took their orders to enjoy elsewhere.

Camille kept a close eye on each one.

Watching people, studying their movements, their expressions, their body language, had been a habit engrained in her as an FBI profiler. Though it had been some time since she used the skill in any official capacity, she instinctively applied it to every situation she found herself in. Camille was once afflicted with the notion that she could break down a person's entire psychological make-up within two minutes of meeting them. These days she wasn't nearly as confident. But it didn't stop her from trying.

She knew, for instance, that the middle-aged couple sitting two tables away was in the midst of a relationship crisis that the French bistro cheeriness of the City Perk did little to alleviate. His wandering eye was most certainly to blame. Her blatant indifference didn't help. That wandering eye landed on Camille, as it had every other woman who walked into the café. A couple of the younger girls met the handsome man's gaze with passive smiles and that unmistakable lock-of-hair-tucked-behind-the-ear signal of flirtation. Camille responded with the thousand-yard stare indigenous to prison yards across the country and perfected through her eight years spent in the company of the planet's most hardened criminals.

No great surprise that his eyes failed to find her a second time.

She was used to the attention, even before the tabloids made her face a fixture in hair salons and hospital waiting rooms across America. When it came to her appearance, Camille could be self-effacing to a fault; meeting most compliments she received with a sneer, a sigh, or an eye roll. On really good days an unsuspecting suitor got all three. But the compliments kept coming. Even after a bullet fragment cut across her left cheek, dotting her olive complexion with a one and a half-inch scar, no Camille Grisham news story was ever complete without at least one reference to what they termed her 'fashion runway' looks. The last story even went so far as to suggest that she play herself in the movie version of her life, since very few actresses on the current SAG roster could fit the bill. Little that Camille read about herself inspired genuine laughter. That last bit certainly did. Unfortunately, it didn't make the glare of the spotlight any less harsh.

The stares from admirers and curious onlookers were easy to deal with. Sometimes they pointed, sometimes they took pictures with their cell-phone cameras, but they always did so at a respectful distance.

The cold, hungry stares of the media sharks were something else altogether. There was no casual curiosity with them; no respectful distance. The sharks only wanted blood, and in six months of pursuing Camille's story they had gotten plenty. But true to every shark's nature, it was never enough. No matter how many sound bites they got, they wanted more. No matter how dutifully her ex-police sergeant pit-bull of a father fought them off, they found a way to slip past him. No matter how bright and festive the atmosphere around her was, they managed to darken it.

The man sitting near the café entrance was just such a shark. Camille knew it the moment he walked in, though his humble smile, weathered tweed jacket, and crisp blue linen shirt offered an admirable disguise. Despite making a concerted effort not to look in his direction, she could sense that he had been watching her. His attention was subtle – passing glances mostly – but it was persistent. When she finally returned his attention with the hardest glare she could summon, he shifted nervously in his chair and promptly looked away. The real sharks rarely looked away, and for a moment Camille wondered if she had misjudged his intentions. Perhaps he was nothing more than the young English Lit professor that his attire suggested him to be. Or maybe it was a rare case of the prey finally getting the best of the predator. Either way, Camille couldn't help but feel relieved when he stood up, took one last pull from his coffee cup, and hoisted his messenger bag around his shoulder.

The thousand-yard death stare strikes again, she thought as she allowed an easy smile to spread across her face. That stare was by far the most effective weapon of defense that she had, and she didn't even need a license to carry it.

Once he was out of sight, Camille turned her attention back to the unhappy couple. The husband's eyes were now firmly planted in a newspaper while his wife's eyes drifted impassively out the window. She was very pretty; elegant yet understated. But behind the carefully constructed veneer, Camille saw a broken woman. A woman not unlike herself. But unlike Camille, there appeared to be no fight left in her; no death-stare capable of combating the predators. She didn't know what tragedies may have stained this woman's past, but she was well aware of the tragedies that stained her own. She lived with them every day. Yet she still had the will to fight, and the strength to push back when she needed to. That strength wasn't always easy to come by, and Camille would need a lot of it in the days and weeks ahead, but she was confident it would be there.

She found herself staring at the woman in an effort to get her attention. She had little more to offer than a smile and a nod of understanding, but she hoped that the quiet acknowledgement from a kindred spirit would be enough to help her find the resolve to look beyond the black hole of despair that passed for her husband.

Unfortunately, her gaze was not enough to break the spell of whatever daydream the woman had retreated into.

It was enough to attract her husband, however. His eyes narrowed as they fell on Camille and she could sense the makings of a smile come across his chemically tanned face.

Camille smiled too as she imagined his reaction to the stiff middle finger she was about to shoot in his direction. She was on the verge of pulling the trigger when something diverted her attention.

The man with the messenger bag was approaching her table.

Suddenly forgetting about her crusade against Mr. chemical-tan, Camille grabbed her coffee mug and stood up. She had been right about the shark's intentions all along and was upset with herself for not leaving the moment she saw him.

Her abrupt movement caused him to stop a few feet short of the table. He smiled as he extended his hand.

Camille stopped him before he could begin the pitch for whatever it was he wanted to sell. "Sorry, I was just leaving."

He blocked her path as she tried to walk away, still trying to disarm her with his less-than-charming smile. "Just a quick moment of your time. That's all I ask."

Resisting her first instinct to shove him into the table, Camille rigidly stood her ground. "If you start by telling me you're with the Post or the Mile-High Dispatch, that moment will be quicker than you can possibly imagine."

"I promise I'm not with either one. My name is Jacob Deaver and I should say, in the interest of full disclosure, that I am a former journalist with the Boston Globe. *Former* being the operative word. No respectable news agency would touch me with a ten-foot pole now."

"And this is supposed to make me feel *better* about talking to you?"

He chuckled nervously. "Probably not. But I swear my intentions are good."

"A journalist with good intentions. That would certainly be a first."

"That's precisely why I left journalism."

"If you aren't angling for a story then why are we talking?"

"I never said I wasn't angling for a story. I merely said I wasn't an active journalist."

His voice was laced with a know-it-all smugness that reminded Camille of the college kids who usually occupied the café. Despite his thick beard and conservative appearance, he probably wasn't much older than any of them. He certainly wasn't any more tolerable to be around. "Did you come in here with the intention of invading my personal space or did the notion just randomly strike you?"

The self-assured grin he fought to maintain suddenly abandoned him and the hand he had prepared to extend fell into his pocket. "I didn't follow you here if that's what you're suggesting."

Camille didn't believe him but saw no benefit in belaboring the point. "Either way I don't have time to chat. And even if I did, it wouldn't be with some kid who has nothing better to do than waste his time pursuing a story that has already been told a million times."

"I'm not a kid, Ms. Grisham. And I can guarantee this story hasn't been told."

She had been prepared to walk away, but his unwavering tone gave her pause. "What makes you so sure about that?"

"Two minutes. Please." With that, he lowered his messenger bag and pushed a chair back from the table.

Camille watched with wary eyes as he sat down. She continued standing. "Who are you?"

"My name is Jacob Deaver."

"You've already told me your name. But you haven't told me who you are."

"I'm someone who wants to give you an opportunity that no one else has."

She couldn't help but roll her eyes. "And what opportunity would that be?"

"The opportunity to let the world hear from you in an unfiltered, unedited way. Your thoughts, your experiences, your opinions."

"Same spiel I've heard countless times, Mr. Deaver. Still not interested." Camille turned to walk away, but the words he said next stopped her cold.

"What if I told you that a major publisher has solicited Daniel Sykes for the rights to his authorized biography?"

"I'd say that has absolutely nothing to do with me and I'd keep walking," she answered in a voice that came dangerously close to faltering.

"What if I said that it has everything to do with you?"

Camille suddenly felt the urge to sit. "Then I guess I'd ask you to explain."

Jacob cleared his throat as if he were about to recite a rehearsed speech. "I'm a former employee of the publishing house behind the book and I personally know the author who has been hired to write it. It's going to be published, Ms. Grisham. And the timetable for getting it to press is very short."

"How short?"

"Five, maybe six months at most."

"And you said this is an authorized biography of Daniel Sykes, meaning he has an active role in the project?"

"From what I understand, he has been corresponding with the author for at least three months. Sykes had apparently lobbied for in-person interview sessions, but the prison refused to sign off on it." He smiled. "I don't think the author was too keen on the idea either."

Camille failed to see the humor. "Explain what you meant when you said this has everything to do with me."

Jacob's smile went away. "You might want to sit down."

"I still haven't decided whether or not this conversation is worth my time."

"Fair enough. The book was originally designed to be a tell-all of Sykes' life, from his childhood through the present. But during the process of creation it was decided that the focus should be narrowed."

"Narrowed to what?"

"His capture. Specifically, the role that you and Agent Andrew Sheridan played in that capture."

Camille's legs felt wobbly and she could no longer fight the urge to sit. "What are you talking about?"

"Based on what I've heard, Sykes has no plans to discuss the details of his murders, the reason he committed those murders, or anything else related to his past. He only agreed to do the book if you and Agent Sheridan were the featured topics."

"How could they allow him to do that?" Camille asked, as if she hadn't already known the answer.

"Apparently there was some initial opposition to the idea, mostly fueled by fear of a libel lawsuit. But ultimately there was too much money to be made not to go forward. Same sad story as always."

Camille had been fully prepared for the bright atmosphere of the City Perk Café to fade at some point, and that's exactly what happened. What she wasn't prepared for was how dark it would actually get. "So, what's your interest in this?"

"Like I said before, I want you to have the chance to tell your side of the story. Make no mistake, Ms. Grisham, this book will not be objective. The goal is to cast you, Agent Sheridan, and possibly the entire Federal Bureau of Investigation in the most negative light possible. In my opinion there has to be some kind of counterbalance to that."

The mention of Agent Sheridan in the same sentence as 'negative light' almost brought tears to Camille's eyes. Her name had been dragged through the mud in almost every way imaginable. She was used to it and wouldn't lose a moment's sleep if it happened again. But to go after Andrew Sheridan, a man who was a hero by any measure of the word, a man who was no longer here to defend himself, was downright criminal. And Camille knew it was something she absolutely could not let happen. "It will never make it to print. I'll make sure of it."

"I'm afraid that ship is already sailing."

The measured confidence in Jacob's voice shook her. "He has a wife and nine-year-old daughter for Christ's sake. How could someone even think about—"

"I understand that. But what you have to understand is that you have a lot more to lose in this situation than anyone else. If this book is released with even half the garbage that Sykes is trying to put out there, it could seriously stain your reputation. With everything you have going on – Elliott Richmond, the questions about your friend's murder – you can't afford to have anyone undermining your credibility. The best option you have is to go on the offensive; strike down anything that Sykes says before he even has the chance to say it."

"And how am I supposed to do that?"

Jacob hesitated, as if his response was one that he had to pull from the depths of his being. "Write your own book."

Camille bit down on her lip to stop herself from yelling. Of all the ways the sharks had ever attacked her, Jacob Deaver's attack was by far the most brutal. In less than five minutes he'd managed to tap into every vulnerability that she had – Daniel Sykes, Andrew Sheridan, her best friend's murder, and the person responsible for it – and he used it to pitch a book. Even if everything he said about Sykes was true, Camille didn't believe for one second that he tracked her down out of some altruistic need to save her reputation. He saw an opportunity to build his own.

"I think your two minutes are up."

Jacob's hooded eyes widened. "Ms. Grisham, please hear me out. I've read everything there is to read about your story. I know you tried to save your partner. I know you tried to save those two girls that Sykes ended up killing. But the people behind this book are going to say something very different. How do you think it's going to be for the families of those victims to hear only one version of the story? *His* version of the story? It will be devastating. You have the opportunity, right now, to stand up for their belief that you did everything possible to save the people they loved. You have the opportunity to confirm what you and I both know is the truth. For your sake, for the sake of those families who are still mourning, don't let that opportunity pass."

In Camille's mind she was screaming at him, throwing coffee mugs, pushing over tables, calling him every obscene name imaginable. When she opened her mouth to actually speak, she could only manage the faintest of whispers. "Goodbye, Mr. Deaver."

As she stood up from the table he gently grabbed her hand. Aside from the fact that he was a stranger, something about his touch made her recoil.

"I know this has probably been a lot to take in, and I apologize if you feel ambushed. That was honestly the last thing I wanted to do. But everything I'm telling you is true, as is my sincerity in wanting to help you. Perhaps with the benefit of time you'll be able to see that. If you do and would like to talk more about it, I'm staying at the Brown Palace Hotel." He reached into his coat pocket and pulled out a piece of paper on which he had already hand-written a telephone number. "You can call the front desk and they'll connect you to my room. I'd be happy to meet with you whenever, wherever. All I ask is that you consider it."

Camille studied the paper a moment longer than she intended to. The hesitation bothered her. "There's nothing to consider," she replied, hopeful that the sudden doubt in her heart did not reveal itself in her voice. Then she took a deep breath, cast one last glance at the French Bistro cheeriness of the City Perk, and walked away from Jacob Deaver.

When she reached the door, she looked back at him. The hand that he held the paper in was still extended, as if he fully expected her to come back for it.

Much to Camille's horror, she almost did.

CHAPTER TWO

PROS AND CONS

Desperate to take her mind off the unfortunate encounter with her would-be biographer, Camille picked up the notebook the moment she walked into her apartment. It was a seventy-page blue spiral with a wide-rule designed for third graders with sloppy penmanship. The fact that she wasted time dwelling on such trivial details was a big reason why the notebook had remained blank since she bought it two weeks ago. Her flagrant indecision was another.

Camille got the notebook after finishing a lengthy telephone conversation with a man she had every hope of never speaking to again. Special Agent Peter Crawley was an instructor at the FBI Academy and one of the brightest minds in the Behavioral Analysis Unit. He was a mentor and a friend. He was also one of the reasons why she decided to give up her shield.

Crawley had been the Agent-In-Charge of the Circle Killer task force. Camille and Andrew Sheridan were the first two field agents asked to join the effort. When Daniel Sykes was finally apprehended three years later, the number of agents on the task force totaled ninety. Yet in the end, Camille, Sheridan, and Crawley were the only three there when Sykes' terror spree came to an end.

Only one of them emerged with their FBI career still intact.

Agent Sheridan lost his life trying to capture Daniel Sykes. Camille lost faith in herself, the agency she had given eight years of her life to, and a world that allowed monsters like Sykes to even breathe the same air as everyone else. Agent Crawley lost countless hours of his existence trying to convince her not to quit.

But his efforts had ultimately been in vain, just as they had been when he assured the Bureau's top brass that the circumstances surrounding Agent Sheridan's death could not have been prevented. Crawley knew the truth of what happened in that basement. He knew that Agent Sheridan should not have died. He knew that the two coeds whom Sykes had been holding captive for a month should not have died. But because of his belief in Camille's value to the Bureau, he thought it best to omit that knowledge from his testimony.

The review board ultimately agreed with his assessment and recommended that she resume active field work immediately. Crawley recommended that she take a long vacation, pay a visit or two to the Bureau head-shrinker, and do her best to leave Daniel Sykes in the past.

Camille chose the third option.

There were plenty of reasons why she had to quit; chief among them was the inescapable fact that every day she entered the BAU offices she would have to look Crawley in the eye, fully aware that he knew the truth. He would have done his best not to judge or think less of her, and for a while he probably would have succeeded. But Camille feared that every reminder of Agent Sheridan's absence would make her presence less and less tolerable, until Crawley's decision to overlook her failure became his biggest regret. There was no one in the Bureau she respected more, and the idea of incurring the wrath of his disappointment was more than her already fragile psyche could have withstood.

She may not have had Crawley's blessing when she tendered her resignation letter, but she still had his admiration; and that admiration would remain as long as she wasn't there to remind him of the agent that he needlessly lost. That assurance was one of the few things that helped her sleep at night.

She had barely closed her eyes in the two weeks since he contacted her.

Despite her recent practice of ignoring every phone call she received from the dreaded 202 area code, Camille took Crawley's call right away. True to his reputation as the most emotionally-barren man on the planet, he didn't waste a second of time with personal pleasantries.

There were four dead girls, he had informed her, all killed with the same pattern of sado-sexual mutilation and all within four months of each other. Camille could almost picture the case file in his hand as he broke down the stats in the infamous monotone that passed for his voice. When Crawley finally asked what her opinion was, Camille told him that she didn't have one. When he pressed, she answered with one word: *copycat.*

There wasn't an ounce of hesitation in his voice when he asked her to come back. No field work, he had assured her. Just hands-off consulting with the current field agents assigned to the case. Crawley was right to think that she couldn't be trusted in the field. He was wrong to think that she could do anything to help him. But with four murders that looked depressingly similar to the ones committed by Daniel Sykes, and a Bureau full of anxious figureheads, Crawley may have felt that he didn't have much choice.

The possibility that someone had decided to pick up where the Circle Killer left off angered Camille in ways she couldn't describe. But she knew there was nothing she could do about it. Why she hadn't told Crawley that right away was a question she couldn't answer. She wanted to. She needed to. But she didn't. Instead, she told him she would need time to consider his offer.

Crawley not so gently informed her that he didn't have the luxury of waiting while she considered his offer. If the copycat held true to Sykes' pattern, the next event could occur within the month, which meant he needed an answer, and he needed it immediately.

No matter how much Camille dreaded the idea of another murder, an immediate answer was something she simply couldn't commit to. This required due deliberation, she told him; an adequate weighing of the pros and cons. The Bureau may have thought it had a lot to gain by bringing Camille back into the fold, but she had even more to lose.

Crawley eventually relented but ended the conversation with yet another reminder of how important her prompt response was.

Camille bought the notebook with the hope that a pros and cons list would help facilitate a quick decision. It didn't. In fact, she was no closer to a resolution now than when she started. And the longer that notebook remained blank, the longer it took to come up with even a single legitimate item to write on the *con* side of the page, the more Camille doubted her ability to tell Crawley no.

She sat at her desk after returning from the City Perk with a pen firmly pressed against the paper, as if the sheer force of her grip would summon the words that had thus far eluded her. An hour later she had nothing to show for her efforts other than a jagged hole in the paper created by the sharp fountain tip. Agent Crawley would have to wait at least one more day for her decision, and if Camille were being honest, she would admit that tomorrow would most likely produce the same result.

Burying the notebook as far down in her desk drawer as she could, she allowed her thoughts to drift back to Jacob Deaver.

Curious to know more about him, she turned to her computer for the requisite Google search of his name. All she managed to find were two Boston Globe articles written in 2011 and 2013 respectively. Standard crime beat material. There were no images of Jacob or other bibliographical references. The results for Daniel Sykes's supposed autobiography were similarly scarce. There was no title, publisher, or author information. If the book was as close to publication as Jacob claimed, there should have at least been some noise on the tabloid sites. But there was nothing.

Camille wanted to take this lack of information as proof that the details Jacob provided were not truthful, or were, at the very least, grossly exaggerated. But she knew that when it came to anything related to Daniel Sykes, there was no such thing as a gross exaggeration.

Given the narcissistic, attention-seeking nature of most serial killers, Sykes' desire to keep himself in the news made absolute sense, as did the timing of the book's release. If he had any inkling of the potential copycat, he would do anything necessary to maintain his stranglehold on headlines that would certainly be taken from him once the details of the crimes became widespread.

There was also the matter of the copycat himself. Much like Sykes, he would be driven, at least in part, by the insatiable need to be noticed, feared, and admired. He would feel a connection to Sykes, but there would also be a natural sense of competition. And if Sykes' book was seen by the copycat as an attempt to up the ante, there was a good chance that he or she would respond in kind.

Careful, Camille. You're starting to sound like a profiler again.

She smiled even though there was nothing funny about the thought. She may have been operating on little more than theory, but the connection between the copycat and Sykes' alleged book was becoming frighteningly clear.

What wasn't clear was the extent of Jacob Deaver's true interest in that book. The scavenging journalist explanation was the easiest one to latch onto. In Camille's experience, however, the easiest explanation was rarely the correct one.

There was something more. It wasn't just his words that told her that. It was the look in his eye; the quiet desperation in his tone. The fact that he'd written down his hotel room phone number prior to their meeting only confirmed what Camille already knew: their encounter was not accidental. That meant Jacob knew she was going to be at the City Perk. And the only way he could have known that was if he had been following her.

It wouldn't be the first time a reporter had done such a thing. Most of them freely admitted to doing so. But Jacob could not have been more adamant in his denial; just as he had been adamant that his motives did not extend beyond a desire to help Camille tell her story.

She couldn't help but question that, but she also couldn't deny her curiosity to learn as much about this book as possible. She began to wonder if she had been too quick to leave the café. Even if the odds were ninety percent that Jacob's story added up to nothing, the remaining ten percent was too significant to ignore.

As she looked up the telephone number of the Brown Palace, Camille told herself that it was about the book and nothing more. But in truth it was about a lot more. It was about a gnawing instinct she couldn't shake. It was about a debt to Agent Crawley that remained unpaid. It was about a murderer whom she felt increasingly compelled to stop.

There was no logical reason to believe that Jacob Deaver could help her achieve any of those ends, but logic was a crutch that she no longer had the luxury of relying on.

She had just picked up her phone to dial the Brown Palace front desk when the cell lit up with an incoming call.

Camille bristled when she saw the word DAD flashing across the screen. This was the fifth time he had called today, and the sixtieth since she'd moved out of his house two weeks ago. Over-protective didn't come close to describing Paul Grisham, especially after the turn his daughter's life had taken in the past six months.

She ultimately couldn't blame him. In fact, part of her welcomed the security that his obsessively-watchful eye brought with it. But the constant questions about the safety of her apartment building, the concerns about adequate street lighting, and the recurring offers to install deadbolts and motion sensors were starting to wear thin. He hadn't been this concerned when she left for college sixteen years ago. Then again, she hadn't been shot and nearly killed less than three months before that move – as had been the case now.

So, as she had done with the previous fifty-nine calls, Camille took a deep breath and smiled before she picked up.

"Hey dad. What's up?"

"Where are you?"

She shook her head at his terseness. "You mean you haven't secretly implanted me with a GPS yet?"

"I'm being serious, Camille."

"I'm home, and I'm perfectly safe," she sighed. "If you want me to check under the bed while I have you on the line—"

"I need you to come over."

"Why?"

"Someone is here to see you."

She struggled to clear the sudden lump in her throat. "Who?"

"It's a bit much to try and explain over the phone. Just drop whatever it is you're doing and get over here."

Paul rarely barked orders, no matter how badly he wanted something done. But when he did, Camille listened.

"I can be there in fifteen minutes."

"Good. I'll see you then."

"Do you at least want to give me a hint of what I'm walking in—"

The beep of a disconnecting call did not allow her to finish the thought.

Camille wanted to take a moment to digest what she had just heard, but there was nothing to digest aside from the near-frantic pitch in her father's voice that was completely foreign to who he was. She could venture a guess as to what was behind it, but these days, speculation only led to dark places. So, she stood up from the desk, grabbed her car keys, and headed for the door without giving the action a second thought.

Her Dodge Charger was parked only a few feet from the apartment building's entrance – a convenience that she gladly paid an extra one hundred dollars a month to enjoy.

But what she saw as she walked outside had instantly rendered it, and everything else around it, completely invisible.

CHAPTER THREE

UPPING THE ANTE

"**B**efore you say anything Ms. Grisham, just know that I was telling the truth when I said I hadn't followed you to the coffee shop."

The tweed jacket that Jacob Deaver wore in the City Perk was missing, as was his messenger bag. But the smile – as inappropriate as any that Camille had ever seen – was still on bright display.

Her shock quickly gave way to anger as she briskly approached him. "What do you think you're doing?"

Jacob stood back on his heels. "I think we can both acknowledge that our first conversation ended prematurely."

Prior to now Camille would have actually agreed with that assessment. Her thoughts were very different now. "Why are you here?"

He looked at her with the eyes of an embarrassed adolescent. "Unfortunately, I didn't know any other way. You left the coffee shop without taking my phone number and I knew there was a lot more to be said – for both of us."

"And your response was to follow me back to my apartment? Were you just going to lurk out here like the creep that you obviously are? Or were you going to wait until someone opened the door, so you could slip inside?"

The expression on Jacob's face flattened. "It's not like that."

Camille stopped a few feet away from him, only now noticing how much shorter he was than her five-foot-nine inches. The height advantage did nothing to mitigate the anxiety that his presence inspired in her. "What is it like, Mr. Deaver?"

"If we're going to work together, I'll have to insist you call me Jacob."

Something that sounded like a laugh escaped Camille's throat. "Work together? I'm two seconds away from calling the police on you."

"There's no reason for that. Besides, I haven't done anything wrong. I haven't touched you, I haven't threatened you—"

"You showing up here isn't a threat?"

44

Jacob continued as if she hadn't spoken. "I haven't raised my voice in anger towards you. I simply want to have a conversation. Since when is that grounds for filing a police report?"

Camille paused to properly frame her response. "Okay, Mr. Deaver. I am telling you right now, in as calm a voice as possible, that I do not want to talk to you in any way, shape, or form, and I am asking you to leave."

Jacob looked around the otherwise empty street. "This is a public place. I'm not really sure where I'm supposed to go."

Camille threw her hands up in frustration. "Fine, *I'll* leave." She brushed against him as she walked past, knocking him off balance. She had intended to do more.

Jacob quickly gathered himself. "Are you really going to let Sykes win again?"

Camille stopped.

"Because if you walk away from me, that's exactly what's going to happen."

"You don't know the first goddamn thing about Daniel Sykes. Or me."

"That's where you're wrong." It was in that moment that Camille first noticed the change; the dark edge that had suddenly settled in over Jacob's face. "I know much more than you think."

Despite her body's pleas, Camille remained where she stood. Her stone-faced silence prompted Jacob to continue.

"I meant everything I said back in the coffee shop. I truly want to help you. People need to hear your story. The full truth of it, not the spoon-fed nonsense they're getting from the media. At this point you probably don't think my intentions are anything beyond self-serving. I suppose in some sense you'd be right. But there are others aside from myself that I'm serving. And they have expectations that I can't fail to deliver on; expectations I *won't* fail to deliver on. That's why I'm here. Not because of me. Not even so much because of you. But because of them."

"As far as I'm concerned, all of you can go to hell. Because whatever it is you want from me isn't going to happen. That opportunity went right out the window the moment you decided to follow me home. Now, if I were you, I wouldn't press my luck by staying here any longer."

The smile that came across Jacob's face did little to brighten it. "Oh, that's right. You were going to call the police. I still think it's silly and completely unnecessary, but I guess that's your prerogative. It's funny that it would even cross your mind though, considering the fact that they despise you."

Camille stiffened.

"This stuff you're involved in with the mayor's husband has the entire department under scrutiny from what I understand. Two homicide detectives shot. One killed. And a lot of people are saying it's because of you."

"And I suppose these people failed to mention that my best friend was murdered too."

Jacob nodded. "I'm aware of that, and my condolences go out to you and her family. I know the pain of that kind of loss all-too-well. But you've also experienced your share, which is why I figured you would be more sympathetic to my cause."

"I don't know anything about your cause. All I know is that you're trying to write a book and you need my help to do it. Help you are not going to get."

"My cause is much greater than a book."

"In that case, I wish you double the luck with it. Just make sure I don't see you again."

As if a switch had suddenly been turned on, Camille felt her legs spring to life and she quickly made her way to her car, once again brushing past him as she did.

Jacob walked up to the car as she climbed inside and started it. He had just opened his mouth to speak when he was interrupted by the roar of the engine. When she saw that he was preparing to speak again, Camille put a heavy foot down on the accelerator, filling the air with the sound of 100 crackling decibels.

He spoke as she pulled away from the curb, his words barely audible over the den of engine noise. But she was able to read his lips, and though she had become something of an expert at the art form during her academy training, she hoped that the skill had failed her in this instance.

"Don't worry, Camille. You will," was what she had interpreted his last words to be.

CHAPTER FOUR

CLOSING THE DEAL

The red and white license plate of the Toyota Camry parked in her father's driveway indicated that the car was a rental. Her first thought when she received the call was that Agent Crawley had made a surprise trip in an effort to expedite her decision. She had dismissed the thought as quickly as it came. Now, as she stared at the rental, she couldn't help but wonder.

If Crawley had made the long trip here unannounced, it meant that the situation with the copycat was worse than Camille realized. It also meant that she would have to look him in the eye to tell him no when he asked for her help; something she knew for a fact that she wouldn't be able to do.

Damn it.

Seeing no need to continue her uphill battle against the inevitable, Camille quickly made her way up the driveway and into her father's open front door, not giving herself any time to think about what she would say to Crawley or what he would say to her.

"Just go in there, accept your Bureau visitor's badge, and get it all over with," she muttered to herself, her quiet tone laced with resignation.

She knocked on the screen door as she walked through it. "I'm here dad," she announced before she saw anyone. "I would have been here sooner, but I had an unfortunate run-in with..." She froze at the sight of the woman sitting on the couch. "Oh, hello."

The woman's heavy eyes lit up as she stood. "Hello."

Camille looked at her father, suddenly confused. "Hey dad."

"Hi Camille," Paul Grisham said, rising to his feet. He looked flustered.

"Your phone call sounded urgent. What's going on?"

Her eyes drifted back to the woman. The tall, slender brunette was dressed in a beige Anne Klein business suit. Camille had the same suit hanging in her closet; a holdover from her Bureau days. But this woman wore it much better. A matching clutch was tucked tightly under her arm, as if she was wary of putting it down. Were it not for the purse, Camille would have immediately tagged her as FBI. But the designer accessory, along with her nervous demeanor, made it clear that she was something else.

Paul approached his daughter while the woman stood frozen. His six-foot-three-inch frame momentarily blocked her from Camille's view.

He gave her a light hug. "Thanks for coming so quickly."

"Based on your tone I knew I didn't have much of a choice." She looked past her father to the woman, who was holding her purse even tighter now."

"I suppose an introduction is in order," Paul said as he stepped aside. "Camille, this is Meredith Park. Ms. Park, this is my daughter Camille."

Despite her obvious nerves, Meredith was quick to extend her hand. "Hello."

"Hello, Meredith. I understand you're here to see me." Camille's handshake was cautious.

"I am."

"Ms. Park arrived this morning from New York," Paul added.

"Do we know each other?" Camille asked with genuine confusion.

"We've never met before. But you may have met someone close to me. He's the reason I'm here."

"Go on."

Meredith opened her purse with unsteady hands. "As your father said, I'm from New York City. I run a boutique literary agency out there." She gave Camille a business card for *Park and White LLC*.

A literary agency. The finely embossed card stock suddenly felt like a fifty-pound weight in Camille's hand. She handed it back without saying a word.

Meredith took the cue to continue. "I represent a true-crime author named Jacob Deaver. He is in the process of writing a book and he may have attempted to contact you about it."

Camille's expression darkened. "So, I have you to blame for that."

Meredith seemed caught off guard by the sharp reply. "You talked to him?"

"Yes, I did. No less than twenty minutes ago."

A wave of relief washed over Meredith's porcelain face. "Oh thank God."

"It's nice to know that you're so excited about it. But I should inform you that I almost called the police on him."

"What?"

"What do you mean you almost called the police?" Paul said in the pit-bull tone that Camille had come to know all-too-well.

"He's been following me."

Meredith shut her eyes as if she were struggling to process Camille's words. "For how long?"

"I'm not sure. All I know is that this morning I went to a coffee shop two blocks from my apartment and from out of nowhere he approaches my table trying to pitch his book idea. I politely declined the offer and left. Then I get the call from my dad telling me to come over, and guess who I run into outside my apartment building?"

Meredith's breath caught. "It just doesn't sound like him to be that aggressive."

"Trust me, he's that aggressive."

"What did he do?" Paul asked. His tone made Camille grateful that Jacob was nowhere in the vicinity.

"The same thing he did in the coffee shop. Only this time he wasn't so quick to take no for an answer."

"Did he threaten you?"

"No dad, it wasn't anything like that." She turned to Meredith. "But you need to know that your client is a certified creep."

"I don't know what to say about that. I've never known him to be that way." She paused to blow out a deep breath. "I'm just happy to know that you've seen him."

Camille's eyes narrowed. "After hearing everything I just told you, how could you possibly be happy?"

Meredith waited a long beat before answering. "Because he's been missing for almost three weeks."

Unsure that she heard the words correctly, Camille turned to her father for clarification.

"That's why she's here," he concurred.

Camille felt something tighten in her chest; the instinct that she had felt before but suddenly wanted to ignore. "The Jacob Deaver I saw looked pretty damn alive and well, so maybe you should explain what you mean by missing."

Meredith looked at Paul. "Do you mind if I sit?"

"Absolutely," Paul replied as he pointed her to the couch.

"Jacob has been working on a book about Daniel Sykes for the past few months. He-"

"Wait," Camille interrupted. "*Jacob* is the one working on the Sykes biography?"

Meredith eyed her quizzically. "Yes. If you met with him, I figured you would have known that."

"He told me that someone else was writing the Sykes book."

"Someone else? Who?"

"He didn't give me a name. He only said it was a friend."

"Well that's certainly news to me."

"And is it also news to you that the book is scheduled to be released in the next few months? Because he seemed pretty confident that it would be."

"I can assure you that isn't true."

Camille let out an exasperated sigh. "And Jacob's author friend?"

"As far as I know he doesn't exist. Not as Sykes' biographer anyway."

"So, he was lying to me the entire time."

"I'm really confused," Meredith confessed. "The entire purpose of him coming out here was to tell you about his work on Sykes' book and to ask you to be a part of it. Why would he claim that someone else was writing it?"

"I don't have an answer for that. All he said was that the book was going to be filled with inflammatory information about myself and the FBI and he wanted to write a book about me as a means of counteracting that. It all sounded perfectly noble. Unfortunately, I had a difficult time believing it. Now I know I had good reason."

"It just doesn't sound right. None of it does."

Camille noted the hint of panic that came across Meredith's face as she rose from the couch and began pacing the room.

"Why don't we go back to what it is that brought you here?"

Meredith stopped pacing long enough to collect her thoughts. "Perhaps it's best if I start from the beginning."

Camille sat down on the couch. "Please do."

"Jacob has been working on the Daniel Sykes biography for well over a year now. The original intent of the book was to paint a more three-dimensional portrait of Sykes' life. We all knew about the horrific things that he'd done, and the psychosis that must have driven those actions. What we didn't know was where he came from, what influenced him, what other forces existed in his life – good or bad – that made him who he was. How were the people in his life affected? There were certainly people who knew Sykes to be someone else and loved that version of him. What did they have to say about what kind of man he was? What kind of child he was? Were there any indications that he was capable of what he ultimately did? Was there any way he could have been helped before he did it? That was the story that Jacob wanted to tell."

Camille's face burned with anger. "He killed twenty-seven people. He's rotting in a prison cell where he belongs awaiting execution. End of story. Were you trying to turn him into some kind of sympathetic character? Some poor victim of circumstance who was merely a product of his terrible upbringing?"

"Absolutely not. Believe me, Jacob was not interested in writing a sympathy piece, and I wasn't interested in reading one. He simply wanted to dig into his past, talk to the people who knew him best. He'd made several trips to Sykes' hometown in the hopes of doing that. He spoke with Sykes' estranged wife, his father, even the pastor of the church he grew up in. No one was willing to talk."

"I can sure as hell understand why," Paul barked.

"The project was at a complete standstill," Meredith continued. "It had gotten to the point that I was trying to figure out how I was going to recoup the publishing advance that Jacob had been paid." Meredith paused. "Then I came up with an idea that I thought would salvage the project."

"And what idea was that?" Camille asked.

Meredith hesitated, as if she needed to work up the courage to answer. "Shifting the focus of the book from Daniel Sykes to you."

Camille bit down on her lip to stop herself from yelling. "So, it was your idea to drag my name, the Bureau's name, through the mud. And for what? To sell a few goddamned books?"

Meredith held up her hands. "That wasn't the intention, by either me or Jacob. We wanted to give you a forum to tell your story as you experienced it. There have been plenty of reports about what happened the day you captured Sykes, but no one really understands the toll it's taken on you since. Not to mention the ordeal you had to endure immediately after with your friend being murdered and the ongoing fallout from that. There is a lot to your story, Camille. We simply wanted to tell it."

"Jacob outlined his pitch the exact same way. But he also told me that the book he wanted to write was a direct response to the Sykes book which was going to portray me and the Bureau negatively. Is that true?"

"That was never the original intent of the book. I swear."

"Then why would he tell me that?"

"Unfortunately, I can't offer a good answer to that except to say that he wasn't telling you the truth, which I don't understand because that's not the kind of person he is."

"He certainly could have fooled me."

Paul interjected. "So, you were the one who suggested he fly out here to approach Camille with this book idea."

"I was actually there when he booked the plane ticket."

"Had you kept contact with him since?"

"The last time I spoke to Jacob was the day after he arrived here. That was nineteen days ago. He told me that he had conducted a couple of internet searches and came up with this address as your last known residence."

"A couple of internet searches?" a wide-eyed Paul cut in. "Please tell me it's not that easy for a stranger to find out where I live."

"I'm sorry to tell you dad, but it's that easy," Camille replied.

Meredith continued. "He said that he had seen you and your father loading some moving boxes into your car. He was going to approach you then, but he didn't feel it was the right time. He said he would wait a day or so and get back to me with an update. That was the last time I heard from him. I must have called his cell phone fifty times since. He never answered. When I called the hotel he was staying in, the clerk told me he had checked out after one night. He isn't married, he doesn't have a girlfriend that I'm aware of, and I didn't have any family contacts. So, all I could do was sit on my hands and wait to hear something."

"You didn't think to call the police?" Camille asked.

"I called them, along with practically every hospital in the state. There was no sign of him, and the police told me that without any evidence that he had been here beyond his one-night stay at the hotel, there wasn't anything they could do."

"So, after not hearing from him for nearly three weeks, what made you come out here now?"

Meredith took a labored breath as she reached into her purse and pulled out her cell phone. After scrolling through it for a moment, she handed it to Camille. "Because last night I received this."

Camille took the phone. The email message on the screen had been composed yesterday afternoon at 2:42 P.M. The subject line consisted of only two words: *Camille Grisham.* The body of the message consisted of three short sentences:

Meeting at Grisham residence tomorrow at 10:30 A.M. Closing the deal. Need you there.

"Jacob wrote this?" Camille asked as she continued studying the perplexing message.

"Apparently so," Meredith answered without much confidence. "I don't recognize the email address, but most people I know have more than one."

"Did you write back?"

"Several times. No response. Then I tried his cell phone."

"And?"

"Disconnected."

Perhaps that explained why Jacob offered the number to his hotel instead of a personal one. The tightness in Camille's chest returned. "You realize there was no meeting scheduled here today, right?"

"I realized that before I left New York."

"So why do you think he sent this?"

Meredith let out a nervous chuckle. "Since you were apparently the last person to talk to him, I'm hoping you can tell me."

"I don't know much beyond what I've already told you. Before we ended our first meeting, he told me he was staying at the Brown Palace and tried to give me the phone number to his hotel room in the event I wanted to discuss his proposal further. But I didn't take it."

"The Brown Palace?" Meredith said with mild surprise. "As far as I knew he had been booked at a Doubletree near the airport."

"I'd call that a fairly significant upgrade," Paul chimed in with a light smirk.

"Considering his fledgling author status, I'd say the same thing," Meredith added.

"So, you don't hear from Jacob for the better part of three weeks, then out of the blue you receive this cryptic message telling you to fly out here to meet him."

"On the same day he approaches you for the first time," Paul said to Camille. "That obviously isn't coincidental."

"Then what is it?" a visibly concerned Meredith asked.

Camille hesitated before answering. The tightness in her chest, the intuition, told her exactly what she needed to say, but she knew how dire the consequences would be once she said it. She had only known Meredith Park for a short time, but she wanted nothing more than to spare her the pain that she knew was an inevitable consequence of a truth only she was willing to give voice to. But there could be no hesitation. Just like there would be no sparing of pain.

"Do you happen to have a picture of Jacob?"

Meredith once again reached inside her purse. "I brought one in the event I would have to show it to the police." She handed over the wallet-sized photo.

As Camille stared at the bright, smiling face of a man whom she had never seen before, the tightness in her chest began to subside. In its place came a surge of adrenaline that both fueled and frightened her. "We have to go to the Brown Palace. Right now."

"Why? What's the matter?" Meredith asked in a voice that was riddled with shock.

"We have to find Jacob Deaver. And the man I met this morning might be the only person alive who knows where he is."

CHAPTER FIVE

DELIVERY

After an intense round of negotiations that bordered on hostile, Paul reluctantly agreed to remain on standby at the house while Camille and Meredith made the drive to the Brown Palace. He imagined her making the trip in record time, given the HEMI V8 engine that powered Camille's car and her penchant for using that engine to exceed every posted speed limit that she came across.

This would mark the second time in four months that he waited behind while she made a dangerous trip. The first instance resulted in her being shot. Though the circumstances of this instance appeared to be very different from that one, the sense of dread that coursed through his veins was just as potent.

Unlike before, when he was completely powerless to help, Paul made sure this time that he was prepared should his services be required. The twenty-six-year DPD veteran knew a thing or two about running backup and had all of the required tools at the ready, from the address of the Brown Palace Hotel, to Meredith Park's cell phone number, to the signal of the GPS tracker that he had installed on Camille's cell phone before she moved out of the house. The moral implications of secretly installing such a tracker on his adult daughter's cell phone were not lost on him, and he long ago resolved to access it only in an emergency. As far as this protective father was concerned, every moment she was outside his immediate field of vision qualified as an emergency, but he had yet to give in to the instinct to turn it on. Someday he would feel comfortable enough to deactivate the tracker altogether.

But this was not that day.

A trip to his gun safe provided the last and possibly most important tool he would need. The Glock 9 had been a holdover from his department days. It was easy to carry, had a minimal kickback, and rarely ever missed its target – even if that target had never been anything more formidable than a paper bullseye.

Now all Paul needed to do was sit back and wait. Camille had assured him that if anything about the situation felt uneven, she would contact him. He was also instructed to call the police if he didn't hear from her within a specified time frame. His executive decision to provide artillery assistance came when Camille refused his offer to take the Glock herself. Paul understood her reluctance, given her recent history. Fortunately, his draw was still quick, and his hesitation was non-existent.

Of course, he tried to convince himself that it would never come to that. If he thought for a second that such a scenario was truly possible, he would never have let Camille and Meredith go without him, despite his daughter's ability to convince him that she didn't need a watchful eye on her every moment of every day, and the preternatural instincts that told him otherwise.

His nervous pacing began the moment they left the house and hadn't slowed in the hour since. There were attempts to occupy time with one or another of the DIY projects that he had undertaken in the two weeks since Camille moved out. But he couldn't focus on anything other than her for more than a few minutes.

You can't protect her from everything evil in the world, Paul silently reminded himself; the same as he always did when the thoughts became too overwhelming to manage. *Even if you could, she doesn't need it.*

It was with this mantra repeating itself in his mind that he heard the first knock on the front door. It was a single knock. Easy to miss had his senses not been on heightened alert. His mind instantly went quiet as he heard the second single knock, this one softer than the first. The third knock caused his heart to skip. The fourth, a heavy thud that shook the walls of the foyer, made him reach for the Glock.

A near deafening silence followed as he slowly walked to the door.

Paul listened before reaching for the doorknob. He heard nothing but the sound of distant cars and barking dogs and immediately took in a deep breath of relief. The sound of shuffling feet on the front porch cut off his air supply before he could let the breath out.

He held the Glock behind his back as he opened the door. The only thing he saw was the UPS truck parked in front of his house. The driver sat behind the wheel, making a notation in his clipboard. When he spotted Paul, he gave a quick wave, then drove off.

The air returned to his lungs in short, quick bursts as he set the gun down on the foyer table. The eight by ten-inch photo-sized box that the driver left behind rested against the screen door. Paul looked at it for a moment before making a move to retrieve it. The plain white shipping label was addressed to Camille. No return label or additional markings.

The box was light, weighing next to nothing in his hand. A quick shake gave no clue to the contents inside.

The sigh of relief that began two minutes ago was finally completed.

"Guess I'd better remind Rich to use the doorbell next time."

Paul chuckled as he put the box down next to the gun, a gun he was now thoroughly convinced he didn't need.

He left it behind as he walked into the kitchen to use the phone. It had been over an hour since Camille left and he figured the time had come for a status update. He would save the story about his near-fatal run in with the UPS driver for another conversation.

He was just about to dial the last digit of her cell phone number when the front door opened.

That was a quick trip, Paul thought as he promptly stopped dialing. *Oh well, better to get that status report in person anyway.*

In the two seconds it took for him to hang up the phone and turn around, the light smile on his face had morphed into something much, much darker.

CHAPTER SIX

THE CATALYST

The massive Brown Palace Hotel lobby was teeming with afternoon guests. Some of them were checking in and checking out, some of them were enjoying tea and gourmet scones in the opulent dining area, some of them were complaining that their towel warmers were set too high. All of them were very eager, very wealthy, and in Camille's mind, very annoying. The only thing she wanted was to get to a desk clerk to ask for Jacob Deaver's room number, but after a full twenty minutes of waiting, there were still six people ahead of her.

Meredith's naturally elegant air helped her fit right in with the elite crowd surrounding them. But as each dreadfully long minute bled into the next, the cracks in her graceful armor began to show.

"This is absolutely absurd. We can't stand here all day."

Camille eyed the three desk clerks working feverishly to process the heavy traffic flow. She knew they were doing their best and hated the fact that she was about to add significantly to the stress of their day.

"We're not standing here a minute longer," she declared as she grabbed Meredith by the elbow. "I just hope you don't embarrass easily."

"What are you talking about?"

Meredith's question was quickly answered as Camille pushed the two of them to the front of the line.

The glares and hisses were immediate and forceful.

"Are you out of your mind?" barked the silver-haired man at the front of the line who was obviously the master of some corporate universe. "Just what do you think you're do—"

Camille's death stare quickly ended his protest.

The young female desk clerk was quiet but clearly flustered as they approached.

"We're really sorry about the disruption here," Camille said with genuine contrition. "But this is something of an emergency."

"You're gonna have an even bigger emergency if you don't get back in line," a random voice yelled out. Camille pretended not to hear it.

"Ma'am there are other guests ahead of you," the clerk said in a firm but professional tone. "I understand the wait is unusually long today, but we're doing the best we can to—"

"I don't think you understand," Camille interrupted. "There may be someone very dangerous staying at your hotel right now. And it's imperative that we talk to him."

Meredith and the hotel clerk gasped simultaneously.

"What do you mean by dangerous?" the clerk asked. Camille imagined that Meredith was asking the same question.

"Jacob Deaver is the name he may have registered under. Could you look it up please?"

The clerk swallowed hard. "Are you with the police?"

Meredith eyed Camille curiously. Camille eyed her back. *I hope you don't embarrass easily.*

"Yes," Camille answered as she leaned into the desk. "But for the sake of not panicking your guests, we'd rather not have to produce identification."

The clerk blew out a deep breath, nodded, and turned back to her computer. "What was the name?"

"Jacob Deaver." Camille looked at Meredith from the corner of her eye. Thankfully, her poker face was holding up.

"It looks like he's checked out already."

"Checked out already?"

"That's right. A little over an hour ago."

Meredith looked concerned. Camille couldn't blame her.

"Can you tell us which room he was staying in?"

The clerk checked the computer. "307."

"What about the credit card he used," Meredith asked, hints of panic rising in her voice. "What was the name on it?"

The clerk hesitated. "I'm sorry ma'am, but that's privileged information. Even if you are with the police, I'm not allowed to—"

Camille cut her off. "That's okay. We don't need it."

The clerk continued working the computer. "I am seeing something here though. Apparently, he left items behind with another clerk. If you give me a moment, I can ask about it."

Camille nodded as the clerk walked away.

"Checked out?" Meredith's expression was a combination of fear and confusion. The worst combination imaginable.

Camille remained silent as the clerk returned. She was holding two small envelopes.

"As he was checking out, Mr. Deaver told one of the clerks that two women may be coming to see him and he was afraid he would miss them. He said to give them these cards." She looked at the names on the front. "Are you Jessica Bailey and Candace MacPherson?"

Camille's heart plunged into her stomach, taking all of the color from her face with it.

Meredith appeared to sense her distress immediately. "Are you okay, Camille?"

"May I have the notes please?" Camille stammered as she attempted to gather herself.

The clerk handed them over. "Unfortunately, that's all I can offer."

"It's more than enough. Thank you." Camille quickly stepped out of the line and made her way to an empty table in the dining area.

"What just happened back there?" a wide-eyed Meredith asked.

Camille held up the notes. "Do those names look familiar to you?"

Meredith squinted as she glanced at the tiny scribble. "No. Who are they?"

"Daniel Sykes' last two victims."

The color seemed to drain from Meredith's face just as quickly as it had drained from Camille's. "I don't understand."

Camille was slowly beginning to. Her hands were shaking as she opened the note marked *Jessica Bailey*. She read the brief message silently; fearful that giving the words audible life would make them impossible to repeat. When she was finished, she pushed the note across the table.

Meredith briefly studied Camille's face before taking the note. Her expression revealed nothing. After a long pause, she read the message out loud. "*I was failed. My best friend was failed. Our families were failed. Unfortunately, I'm no longer here to speak for myself or for them. But someone can. He will be heard. They all will be heard. Always watching, Jessica Bailey.*"

"What about the handwriting?" Camille asked with a forced measure after Meredith finished reading. "Does it look like Jacob's?"

"Not at all." She handed the note back. "And I'm assuming it wasn't written by Jessica Bailey."

Camille shook her head.

"Then it was written by the man you met today."

Camille didn't respond as she opened the second envelope. The message was exactly the same as the first, except it was signed Candace MacPherson.

"I suppose we call the police now," Meredith said, the gravity of the situation fully evident in her tone.

"I suppose we do," Camille muttered in a voice that was barely audible above the soft harp playing in the dining hall.

They made the walk to the parking garage in silence, both attempting the make their own sense of the situation. When they reached the car, Camille pulled out her cell phone.

"I'd better fill my father in before we make any other moves. I'm sure his nerves are already through the roof."

"That might be an understatement," a male voice said from behind them.

Camille spun back on her heels as Jacob Deaver slowly approached. Only now she knew he wasn't Jacob Deaver.

"Scared. Petrified. Seeing what's left of his life flashing before his eyes. Those might be more apt descriptions of your father's current mental state."

Meredith backed away from the man. Camille walked toward him.

"Meredith? Is this Jacob Deaver?" she asked.

"No, it isn't."

He lifted his arms and crossed his wrists. "Guilty. Guess you'll have to put the cuffs on me now."

As he drew closer, Camille held her ground, already plotting the first area of his body she would strike should it come to that. His thick Adam's apple was a sensible target. "What the hell do you know about my father?"

"Plenty."

"Where is he?"

"It's not really my job to know the 'where'. And frankly I don't care. All I can tell you is that, barring some failed last gasp at heroics, he's still alive." He paused, as if briefly losing himself in a thought. "Which is more than I can say for my sister."

Camille resisted the obvious question, opting instead to unnerve him with her silence. A noticeable quivering of his chin let her know that the tactic had worked.

"And who is my sister you may ask?"

"I didn't ask."

His attention turned to Meredith. "Jacob Deaver asked. He seemed very noble about it all. He said he'd read all the news reports, watched the tearful interviews. But he knew none of it did true justice to Candace's life. Like he knew the first damn thing about Candace's life." He looked at Camille with dark eyes. "Does it make sense now?"

It made perfect sense, but Camille couldn't find the words to communicate that.

He turned back to Meredith. "He bent over backwards to assure my family that the book wasn't about glorifying what Daniel Sykes did. It was merely about understanding him. And in order to understand him, Jacob said he needed to know as much about his victims as possible. My parents were as nice to him as they could be. They're good people. Really good people. But their senses were still dulled by shock. They couldn't see him for the vulture that he really was, even after he insisted on taking pictures of Candace's gravesite. Fortunately, I could see him exactly for what he was."

Tears were running down Meredith's face faster than she could wipe them away. "Where is he?"

"As I said, the 'where' isn't really my concern. I'm more of a 'why' and 'how' kind of person. But the last time I saw him he was lurking outside of Camille's apartment building."

"How did you know he would be outside my apartment building?"

"Because he told me he would be. You see, in the process of intruding on our lives with his heartless questions about my sister's final days on earth, he had somehow gotten the idea that we had become friends. So, I decided to play along, build trust, learn everything I could about his true objective. We exchanged emails. I'd supply him with anecdotes about Candace; he'd give me regular status reports on the book. Since I was the only person he talked to who would actually give him or his book the time of day, he was more than happy to keep me in the loop. The project was going nowhere, as you knew all-too-well, Meredith. Then came the brilliant idea of interviewing Camille. That was your idea, wasn't it?"

Meredith turned to Camille but could barely look her in the eye.

"Yep, I believe it was," the Jacob Deaver imposter continued. "At any rate, he couldn't have been happier to make the trip out here. Told me he'd finally found his bestseller. Having a vested interest in Ms. Grisham's story myself, I couldn't disagree with him. But I also knew it couldn't happen. Not the way he envisioned it anyway. It was bad enough that he wanted to glorify my sister's killer at my sister's expense. Now he wanted to glorify the woman who allowed my sister to be killed. What kind of brother would I be if I allowed that to happen? So, I decided to make the trip out here too."

Camille remained calm as she took another step toward the man she now knew to be Daniel MacPherson, the older brother of Candace MacPherson – one of the two co-eds killed in Sykes' basement on the day he was apprehended.

As far as she knew, Daniel had never been interviewed or photographed, but she did see his name in the 'survived by' section of his sister's obituary. She distinctly remembered the obituary, and the guilt she felt that a young man of only twenty-two would have to endure such an indescribable loss.

Right now, her feelings were very different.

"Do you really think this will honor her memory? Doesn't she deserve better?"

Daniel laughed. "The old mind-fucking technique. I've heard you FBI profilers just love to do that. Of course you aren't an FBI profiler anymore. From my perspective, you were never much of one to begin with."

Camille's reserve of calm had suddenly run out. "Where the hell is my father?"

"Why does everybody keep asking me that? I've already told you, I don't know. What you need to concern yourself with more is who has him."

"Tell me who."

"In due time."

Camille grabbed the smaller man by the shirt collar and threw him against the hood of her car. "Damn it, you're going to tell me now!"

Daniel gasped for air as she squeezed his windpipe. "He's someone just like me, except that killing comes more naturally to him. I've never hurt anyone in my entire life."

Camille squeezed harder. "Bullshit."

"Okay, I've never actually killed anyone. But he has. Four that I know of so far, not counting your father or Meredith's author friend."

When Daniel's eyes began to bulge Camille released her grip. He staggered off the car hood in a desperate search for breath.

Meredith put a hand on Camille's shoulder in a vain effort to comfort her. "We'll find them. Let's just call the police and get this monster locked up first."

Camille pulled out her cell phone and dialed her father's number. She bristled when it went to voice mail. "Jesus dad why aren't you answering?"

"Camille please," Meredith reiterated.

Daniel's face twisted with amusement. "He isn't going to answer. Not now, perhaps not ever. I don't know what the ultimate plan is for him. But I do know what the plan is for you. It's been in the making for a long time now. And this book, this Daniel Sykes love-fest that that piece of garbage Jacob Deaver wanted to write, was the vehicle that we needed. Sykes may have been ultimately responsible, but you were the one who allowed him to roam free. You were the one who could have stopped him. And now you're the one who has to pay."

"And how is she supposed to pay?" Meredith cried. "Hasn't she, haven't you, been through enough already?"

"No, she hasn't been through enough. Not by a long shot. And as far as how she's going to pay? I can't really answer that. I'm merely the messenger. The message has been delivered, which means my work is finished. The ones who can answer your question are the ones you aren't

83

going to see. Not until it's too late anyway." He paused as he turned his now lifeless eyes to Camille. "I wish I had it in me to end you myself. But everyone has their role in life."

"And what is your role?"

"As I've said, I'm merely the messenger."

Jacob smiled wide as Camille dialed 911. It was a hideous smile that reeked of smug satisfaction.

"Are you even going to try to run?" she asked him when she hung up the phone.

"I've done everything I was called to do. It doesn't matter what happens to me now. Besides, the police can't do anything to me that you haven't done one hundred times over." He took a step toward her. "All that matters to me is that you suffer."

His ghastly smile returned. It only took one punch for Camille to knock it clean off his face.

CHAPTER SEVEN

AN OLD FRIEND/ A NEW THREAT

The police had already arrived by the time she made it back to her father's house. The absence of yellow tape meant that they had thus far found nothing to indicate that an actual crime had been committed. It also meant that Camille could breathe a tentative sigh of relief.

She raced up the driveway to the sight of two uniformed officers standing on the front porch. The door was open.

"Did you go inside?" Camille asked the female officer who approached her.

"Yes, ma'am. The house is empty."

"Did you check everywhere?"

"Top to bottom. The front door was open when we arrived. No obvious forcible entry. And it didn't appear as if anything inside was disturbed."

Camille strained her neck to look around the officers and into the house. "Can I go and look around myself?"

"We need to first ask you some questions about—"

Camille had sprinted up the front steps and into the house before the officer could finish her statement. In contrast to the early spring warmth of the air outside, the air inside the house was cold and empty. She rushed into the kitchen then down the stairs into the basement, then outside into the backyard. No sign of her father anywhere. With precious little oxygen remaining in her lungs, she made her way into his office, checking every nook, cranny, and closet along the way. "Dad?" It was as futile sounding a word as she had ever uttered.

Finally, she climbed the staircase, moving quickly past her childhood bedroom and into his. The bed was made with the same crisp edges that he always insisted on. His shoes were stacked neatly in the corner the same as they always were. Her mother's young, smiling face looked at her from a frame on top of the nightstand the same as she always had. Beyond that, there was not a single indicator that her father had ever been here.

Hollow legs carried her back down the staircase. When she reached the bottom, she saw Meredith standing near the front door, her face a sad, quivering mess. Camille imagined her own looked ten times worse.

"He's not here."

"We know," a female voice not belonging to Meredith said.

Camille swung her head to the right as a familiar face stared at her from the kitchen entryway.

"Chloe."

"Hi Camille."

"What are you doing here?" Camille asked wearily, though not because she was unhappy to see her.

Chloe Sullivan was the lead detective in the investigation of her best friend's murder. When the case was intentionally steered in a direction away from the truth, it was Chloe who single-handedly kept it on course. In the process she nearly lost her life – at the hands of the same man who tried to end Camille's.

The bond that formed between them in the aftermath was instant. And though she had lost contact with Chloe recently, she somehow always knew that the detective was never very far away.

Her appearance here only solidified that notion. But it also made Camille unspeakably nervous.

"I'm not here in an official capacity," Chloe said with a thin smile that did little to mask her concern. "I was in my car and I heard the call come in over dispatch. It goes without saying that I got here as fast as I could."

"Thank you," Camille said, though her nerves were no less frayed than before.

"I was getting some background from Ms. Park. She says the man currently in custody claims that your father was abducted."

Camille could only nod.

"She says that her colleague, a man by the name of Jacob Deaver, was also abducted. Presumably by the same person."

"Has he said anything else?" Meredith asked with a shaken voice.

"You mean Daniel MacPherson? As far as I know, he's been uncooperative so far. But the Q&A has only started."

"What am I supposed to do in the meantime?" Camille cried. "I can't just sit here, knowing my father is out there somewhere. Give me another chance with Daniel. I only need a few minutes."

"In your current state I don't think that's a good idea," Chloe advised. "We have plenty of people talking to him now. If there is information to get out of him, they'll find a way to get it." She put a hand on Camille's shoulder. "Is there anything I can do for you now?"

"Aside from finding my father and Jacob Deaver, no." Then she looked Chloe in the eye. "But I do appreciate you coming here."

"Of course. Beyond the fact that Paul is your father, he's also a part of the DPD family. A very important part. That makes this personal for all of us. Me especially. Trust me when I say we'll find him."

Just then, three forensics techs walked through the front door. Two of them fanned out to opposite corners of the house to begin their work while the third approached Camille and Chloe.

"Detective Sullivan. Ms. Grisham."

Chloe smiled. "This is CSI Robert Franklin. I called him and his team in as a special favor."

"Thank you," Camille said to the tech.

"Happy to help, Ms. Grisham. If there is anything here that points the finger at a potential abductor, we'll pick it up."

Camille could only hope that was true as the tech walked away to survey his own corner of the house. She then began her own search; looking for even the slightest thing that might have been missing or out of place. From what she could tell, everything was as it had been before she left for the Brown Palace, right down to her father's car keys and wallet sitting in their usual spot near the kitchen table.

She continued her methodical walk through the house as the CSI techs worked around her. She wasn't sure what they were supposed to find, but she appreciated their presence, as well as the gesture by a good friend that brought them here in the first place. Had the promise to find her father been made by anyone other than Chloe, it would have felt hollow. But Detective Sullivan was as good as they came. And if she promised a positive outcome, Camille had no choice but to believe her.

As she trailed the techs through the house, she was finding very little to sustain that belief. Then she came upon the delivery box on top of the foyer end table. Aside from the fact that it hadn't been here when she and Meredith left the house, what most caught her eye was the plain white shipping label with its crude scribbling of her name. She instinctively reached for it but quickly stopped herself.

"Chloe, come look at this."

The detective rushed over. Her eyes were already fixed on the box. "What is it?"

Camille shrugged. "Apparently it was delivered this afternoon while I was gone."

"Were you expecting a package?"

"No."

Chloe called over her shoulder. "Hey Rob, check this out."

The tech walked over, adjusting his latex gloves. "What is it?"

"We're not sure," Chloe answered. "It was delivered this afternoon."

Robert picked up the small box. "It's light. Feels like paper inside."

"It could be some pictures my dad ordered for all I know," Camille said, not believing one word of it.

"Or it could be something else," Chloe warned.

Camille nodded and held her breath as the tech took out a Swiss Army knife and cut gently along the edge of the box.

"Definitely looks like a piece of paper," the tech confirmed as he peeled back the top. "Odd one, though."

"What do you mean by odd?" Chloe asked, craning her neck to get a better look.

Her question was answered when the tech took out a pair of tweezers and lifted the paper out of the box.

"My God are those blood stains?" Meredith asked, her voice muffled by her hand.

"Four of them," the tech confirmed.

"Spatter?" Chloe asked as she inspected the black page dotted with red.

"No. The pattern is precise, almost as if they came out of a dropper."

"And the names written underneath?"

The tech shrugged. "No idea."

The group turned to Camille.

The four female names were written in white marker, in the same crude penmanship that was evident on the shipping label. Camille didn't recognize the names, but she knew who they were. The phone call that she now knew she had to make to Special Agent Crawley would most likely confirm her suspicion.

There would be no more time to weigh the pros and cons of joining his task force. The copycat had just made the decision for her.

"Do you know what any of this means?" Chloe asked.

"Look on the back," Camille answered in a solemn voice.

Chloe turned the paper over. Beneath the traces of blood that had seeped in from the other side she saw three names written the same as the four on the other side. But unlike those names, the ones she looked at now were very familiar.

Jacob Deaver

Paul Grisham

Camille Grisham

A question mark occupied the space under Camille's name.

"He's leaving his options open for victim number eight."

Silence filled the room while everyone attempted to process Camille's words. But for Camille there was nothing left to process. She knew what needed to happen next. In her heart of hearts, she always knew it would come to this, whether through Daniel MacPherson's design or some other unforeseen circumstance. But she never could have imagined this full circle moment would come with such dire personal stakes.

Daniel Sykes would be most proud of his fledgling protégé, whoever he was. Camille now knew it would be her job to find him. "Would you excuse me for a moment? I have a phone call to make," she said before quietly slipping into her father's office.

True to his reputation as the most emotionally barren man on the planet, Special Agent Peter Crawley didn't waste a second of time with personal pleasantries.

"Let me guess, Camille. You received a note too."

EPILOGUE

MISSION STATEMENT – BY JACOB DEAVER

At least I'm not alone. I take solace in that fact, though perhaps I shouldn't. It is a selfish thought, and considering the circumstances, a completely heartless one. The truth is I wouldn't wish my current circumstance on anyone else in the world.

Paul Grisham is strong. But he is losing his will, much like I am. We have been told that our suffering is not in vain, that it is serving a much higher purpose. The purpose, we are told, is justice. Justice for the twenty-seven people who died needlessly. Justice for the families who continue to grieve over their loss.

But what about our suffering? What about our families?

My original ambition was to write a book about Daniel Sykes, the man who I am told is ultimately responsible for the misery that I am enduring. But my ambitions have since changed. My only purpose now is to stay alive, and the only way to do that is to tell the

Daniel Sykes story the way it should have been told in the first place: through the eyes of those who continue to suffer from his actions.

I have come to learn that theirs is the only truth that matters. Theirs is the only truth worth telling. That truth isn't just about grief and loss and pain. It is about love. It is also about vengeance. Vengeance against the one who allowed it to happen. Vengeance against the one who tried to wash the blood of twenty-seven people off of her hands without thinking anyone would notice.

Someone noticed. And this is his time.

The message I am charged with delivering is very clear. Camille Grisham can no longer run. She can no longer hide. She can no longer keep the truth of who she is from the world.

At least I am not alone here.

But if Camille doesn't step forward to accept the justice due her, I fear that it will not stay that way much longer.

~JD

BONUS CHAPTERS

THE DARKEST
POINT

A GRISHAM & SULLIVAN NOVEL

PROLOGUE

THE GHOSTWRITER

"Is the blindfold too tight?"

I hear this question as I feel hands on the back of my head securing the knot even tighter. The hands belong to a woman, as does the voice. I've only caught glimpses of her here and there. She's middle-aged with blondish hair and tan skin. Her mature, gentle face matches her mature, gentle voice. It's a comforting voice, and I sense that she uses it intentionally. She doesn't come right out and say *everything will be okay, this will all be over soon, just do as he asks and you'll walk out of here alive*, but her constantly reassuring tone implies it.

"It's fine," I tell her, even though it obviously isn't. Because she's trying so hard, I feel an odd compulsion not to make her feel bad. I follow up with, "Thank you."

"You're welcome, Jacob. When you're finished, I'll see about getting you something to eat. You must be starving."

I say nothing this time. I haven't had anything approaching an appetite since I was brought here.

Even though my ability to measure time is pretty much gone, I estimate that it's been nearly three weeks. Aside from the glimpses of a woman whose name I still don't know, I haven't seen much of where I'm being held captive apart from the room I've been locked in. It's a nondescript ten by twelve-foot space with a cot in one corner, a rusted toilet in the other, and a card table and folding chair in the middle. The floor is carpeted, and the walls are painted lime green, so I know it isn't a prison cell. But it may as well be one.

Before each of these blindfolded sessions (of which this is the fifth), I'm instructed through the door to get on my knees and face the wall. The door is opened and two men walk in, one on either side of me. I'm told that if I look at either of them, I'll be shot. I believe them, and I comply. As one man handcuffs me, the other puts the blindfold over my eyes. They then hoist me to my feet and out of the room.

After walking approximately sixty-four steps (I count them as a way of confirming that I'm going to the same place each time), I'm placed in a chair and pushed up to a table. A digital voice recorder is put in front of me. Then the men walk out and the woman walks in. She once referred to one of the men as Robbie, but that's all I know about them. I feel like even that's too much.

Each time, the woman pats me on the shoulder as she walks out and closes what sounds like a heavy door. She does the same thing now. Before she leaves this time, she says, "It's getting a little cold out. I think I'll make soup. Chicken noodle sound good?"

She could be anyone's perfect mother. She could be *my* perfect mother. This makes the nightmare of my situation one-hundred times worse.

After what feels like an eternity of silence, the door opens again, and he walks in. I've come to recognize the sound of his footsteps by now. Not heavy like the two men who are my watchdogs. These footsteps are light and easy. Footsteps that are accustomed to moving through spaces quietly and efficiently. I swallow hard as he pulls back his chair to sit across from me.

"Good morning, Jacob." His voice isn't light and airy like the woman's, but it's mature like hers. Stern and unyielding. "Have you found your appetite yet?"

I clear my dry throat. "Not really."

"We'd like for you to eat. The accommodations may not be much, but the food is fantastic. Besides, how are you supposed to write if you don't fuel your brain?"

I say nothing.

I've come to learn two things about this man so far. The first is that he isn't particularly interested in two-way conversation. He asks questions as a means of making statements, not because he cares about what I'm thinking or feeling.

"Speaking of writing, what do you say we get this session started?" he continues. "We're coming to a fascinating part of the story and I need to get the details out while they're fresh in my mind." With that, I hear the click of the voice recorder. "Do you have any questions before we begin?"

He's never asked me this and I'm not sure how to respond. My question is obvious, or at least it should be, but I'm still afraid to give it voice. Apparently, he senses this.

"It's okay, Jacob. Speak freely."

I attempt to clear my throat again. "I have two questions," I say in a thin, raspy voice.

"Drink this first," he says, and I feel something cold and wet touching my lips.

He tips the bottle and water fills my mouth. I pull at it with frantic chugs until it's gone.

"Better?" he asks when I'm finished.

I nod.

"Good. Now you were saying?"

"I have two questions," I repeat.

"Okay."

"The other man who's here with me. Is he all right?"

"The other man's name is Paul."

"Is Paul all right?"

"You're only asking because you're worried if *you'll* be all right."

He's mostly correct about this. I stay silent rather than lie.

"Paul Grisham is as fine as someone in his circumstance can be. I need him just as much as I need you. Your roles here may be different, but they're equally important."

And that brings me to my second and most important question, the one I'm desperately afraid to ask. He again senses my hesitation.

"What is it you really want to know, Jacob?"

I take in a deep, painful breath and slowly let it out. The air is stale and thick, and it's difficult to breathe. It doesn't help that I'm hyper-aware of every breath I take. When you're not sure which one will be your last, you don't take any of them for granted.

"When you're finished with us, when I help you write your book and Paul does whatever he's supposed to do, will you let us go?"

The question hangs in the air for more than a few seconds before I hear the click of the voice recorder cutting off.

"The short answer is that it may be impossible to let both of you go. But there's a lot that needs to happen between now and then, so for right now, let's stay focused on the task at hand."

I can't see his face, but I can sense his flat, emotionless expression. It's clear to me that he's already formulated the
outcome in his mind, and nothing I say is going to alter that. The only thing I can do now is what I've done from the beginning: comply with everything he asks of me.

When I hear the recorder click again, I know his story is about to begin. And when the story begins, my sole job is to listen. As has happened each of the previous times, when he's finished, I'll be escorted back to my cell (as I said, it may as well be a prison). With one of the watchdogs pointing a gun at my head, the other will remove my blindfold and handcuffs. I'll then sit down at the card table that functions as my workstation, and I'll write; all day, all night, until I've transcribed   every   word   he's   recorded.

So far, his life story has spanned three hundred and twenty typed pages. The end goal of that story, he tells me, is to reveal the truth about the woman whom he feels is responsible for his daughter's murder; the woman whose father is somewhere in this hell along with me. For all I know, the plan is to kill us both. But what differentiates my presence here from Paul's is that his is very personal.

The second thing I know about the man who is keeping me captive, more than anything I've ever known in my entire life, is that he wants Camille Grisham to suffer, and is prepared to go to any lengths to make sure that happens. I fear for myself, but I fear for her and her father even more.

"Now we've come to the part of the story where I tell you about my daughter, sweet, innocent girl that she was. She was murdered by Daniel Sykes, the man who was to be the subject of your book. The man you so desperately wanted to turn into a human-interest story. But he's not a human. He's a goddamn animal. And he killed Madison, my daughter, like a goddamned animal."

I keep every fiber in my body still, too afraid to move or speak.

"But he never should have been allowed to kill her. And make no mistake, he was *allowed* to kill her." He pauses for a long time before continuing. "I need you to listen to this next part very carefully because it involves you. It's the entire reason I brought you here. Are you listening, Jacob?"

"Yes."

I can sense him leaning in until he's a few inches from my face.

"Camille Grisham has to pay in the worst way imaginable. For that to happen, I need you to draw her out."

"Draw her out?" I ask with genuine confusion. "How am I supposed to do that?"

"With your words."

He spends the next several minutes speaking my instructions into the voice recorder, down to the size and style of the font I'm to use in composing the text. The first of the three messages, he explains, will contain the reasons for his actions. The second will serve as the impetus Camille's participation in his objective. The third will be a specific set of instructions for her to follow. Failure to comply with these instructions, he explains, will result in the death of one person every day until she does comply.

After I compose the messages, I'm to make a copy of each and put them in envelopes to be labelled with the addresses that he will supply. My fingerprints, he claims, are a critical piece of the puzzle. From there, we wait for Camille's response.

"Is all of this clear?" he asks as he finally sits back in his chair.

"Yes."

"Good. Now, before you get to it, there's one more thing that I need you to do."

I hold my breath as he stands up and walks behind me.

I keep my eyes shut as he rips the blindfold away from them.

"I think we've officially moved past the stage of pretense. There's no reason you shouldn't know who I am. Open your eyes."

I respond by clinching them even tighter, my mind holding firm to the adage that I've heard expressed in every hostage movie ever made: Never let them show you their face. Once you see their face, you're dead.

Pain as he grabs my hair and yanks my scalp. "Open them!"

I comply. I'm briefly blinded by the LED light from the lamp pointed at my face. The only image I can make out is his silhouette as I blink away piercing strobes of light.

When my eyes finally adjust, I can see the course details of his face.

He smiles at the sound of my shrieking.

After allowing ample time for my shock to sink in, he leans into my ear and whispers. "Time to get to work, Jacob."

CHAPTER ONE

BRIEFING

FBI Special Agent Peter Crawley was all-too-aware of his reputation. Cold. Aloof. Distant. Robotic. He'd even been given a nickname by certain members of the B.A.U. Team: Doctor Ice. It bothered him more than he cared to admit, but he did his best to take it in stride. Deep down, he understood that the moniker was justified. The twenty-three-year Bureau veteran had many strong suits, but emotional engagement wasn't one of them.

So when tough questions arose about a former special agent's decision to join the task force charged with discovering the whereabouts of her missing father, Crawley addressed them with a forced composure that belied his mounting irritation. In addition to being one of the finest profilers he'd ever encountered, Camille Grisham was also a friend, which made the criticism of her inclusion – an inclusion that he'd insisted on – feel very personal.

But because Doctor Ice's well-earned reputation didn't allow him to take such things personally, he had to ensure that his poker face held up, despite persistent badgering from the two local agents assigned to the task force; agents he didn't know, and based on early results, didn't like.

"Look, I understand that she has a long history in Behavioral Analysis and that the two of you are close. But she quit, remember? And based on everything I've heard, she has no desire to come back."

The most vocal of the pair was a hothead named Gabriel Pratt. As profilers went, Pratt was made of all the right stuff. Crawley could see that the moment he laid eyes on him. Subsequent reviews of his personnel file confirmed it. The problem with Agent Pratt was his ego. His was the classic 'big fish in a small pond' syndrome that afflicted many a D.C. hotshot forced to relocate to a Midwest field office too small to handle the weight of their considerable talent.

"I know what's at stake for her, so I don't want to sound insensitive," he continued, "But I'm not sure what she can bring to this investigation beyond her witness statement."

"He's got a point, sir. How do we know she won't let her emotions get the best of her? It's certainly happened before."

Allison Mendoza was Pratt's less-talkative yet equally presumptuous partner. Like Pratt, Mendoza came highly recommended. And like Pratt, she assumed that her opinion was much more relevant to Crawley than it actually was.

"With all due respect to both of you, it isn't your job to understand Camille Grisham. You're here as my CBI liaisons. And while I can appreciate your experience and ability, your involvement here is procedural. In other words, I didn't have a choice. So before you waste another breath questioning Camille's credentials or my judgment, please put your misguided ego aside long enough to understand the actual flow of things here. You're on this task force because the crime occurred in your city. Camille Grisham is on this task force because Director Spaulding wants her to be. The sooner you accept that, the sooner we can all move forward. I want Agent Grisham to feel nothing but welcomed here. Is that understood?"

"*Agent* Grisham," Pratt chided.

"Is that understood?"

Pratt and Mendoza looked at one another, their eyes silently communicating a mutual disdain of Crawley, his condescending tone, and their inability to do anything about it.

"Understood," Mendoza answered, her stare still fixed on Pratt.

"Loud and clear," Pratt concurred, wisely taking his partner's cue.

Doctor Ice breathed an undetectable sigh of relief. "Great. Now can we move ahead with the briefing that brought us here in the first place? Camille is on her way, and I want to make sure we're fully up to speed before she arrives."

He opened his briefcase and pulled out three manila folders, two of which he gave to Pratt and

Mendoza. He opened his and immediately began reading.

"From page two of the report. There are four dead that we know of so far. All women. Two in Pennsylvania, one in Tennessee, and one in Missouri. In each case, the victims were abducted from their homes, taken to a remote location, sexually assaulted, mutilated, and strangled. The mutilation patterns are consistent with those used by Daniel Sykes. As we know, Sykes is in a federal prison awaiting execution. That leaves us with the probability of a serial copycat. We're in Denver because the two latest incidents, the abductions of Paul Grisham and Jacob Deaver, occurred here.

Crawley flipped to the next page of the report. "Daniel MacPherson is the man currently in custody for Deaver's abduction. MacPherson is the brother of Candace MacPherson, Sykes's last victim. Deaver reportedly met MacPherson during his research for a book he was writing about Sykes. The extent of their relationship during that time is unclear, but we do know that at the time of his arrest, MacPherson was posing as Deaver in an effort to get close to Camille. This obviously makes him a prime person of interest in Deaver's disappearance. Unfortunately, we haven't been able to establish a firm connection between MacPherson and the disappearance of Paul Grisham or the previous murders, even though it's safe to assume they're connected. DPD has interviewed him several times to no avail. I'm counting on us to do better.

He flipped to the next page. "There's scant physical evidence aside from the two notes sent to Paul

Grisham's residence and the B.A.U. offices, respectively. The notes were identical in content. DNA from blood found on the paper is a match for Kerrie Wallace and Harley Middleton, two of the victims. But there are no prints, and the writing doesn't match samples taken from MacPherson, Deaver, or Paul Grisham. That basically leaves us at square one."

Crawley closed the report and looked up at Pratt and Mendoza. They were attentive despite already knowing the details of the report. It would have been easy to tune out his summary, but they didn't. He took this as a hopeful sign that they were team players.

"Questions? Concerns?"

"Only about Camille," Pratt said.

Crawley rolled his eyes, the first visible crack in Doctor Ice's armor.

"Specifically, as it relates to our suspect," Pratt clarified.

"Go on."

"She believes that MacPherson is involved in her father's disappearance."

"An assumption we're all making at this point."

"But we don't have the skin in this that she does. Her confrontations with Daniel before his arrest were contentious, and she's already assaulted him once. How do we know she won't go after him again?"

"Jesus, Gabe. Can you blame her?" Mendoza said. "I'd want to beat the hell out of him too. And so would you."

"I'd like to think that if either of us were in that position, we'd have enough foresight to remove ourselves from the situation before it escalated to that point."

"You're telling me that you'd sit on the sidelines if it were your mother or sister out there?"

"I'm telling you that for the integrity of the investigation, I'd have to."

Mendoza laughed. "That's bullshit, and you know it."

"Of course, it's bullshit."

Pratt and Mendoza spun around at the sound of the new voice in the room. Neither of them said a word when they saw who it was.

For his part, Doctor Ice stood up from his desk and smiled, refusing to suppress the overwhelming emotion that this moment inspired in him.

"Good morning, Camille."

Grisham's residence and the B.A.U. offices, respectively. The notes were identical in content. DNA from blood found on the paper is a match for Kerrie Wallace and Harley Middleton, two of the victims. But there are no prints, and the writing doesn't match samples taken from MacPherson, Deaver, or Paul Grisham. That basically leaves us at square one."

Crawley closed the report and looked up at Pratt and Mendoza. They were attentive despite already knowing the details of the report. It would have been easy to tune out his summary, but they didn't. He took this as a hopeful sign that they were team players.

"Questions? Concerns?"

"Only about Camille," Pratt said.

Crawley rolled his eyes, the first visible crack in Doctor Ice's armor.

"Specifically, as it relates to our suspect," Pratt clarified.

"Go on."

"She believes that MacPherson is involved in her father's disappearance."

"An assumption we're all making at this point."

"But we don't have the skin in this that she does. Her confrontations with Daniel before his arrest were contentious, and she's already assaulted him once. How do we know she won't go after him again?"

"Jesus, Gabe. Can you blame her?" Mendoza said. "I'd want to beat the hell out of him too. And so would you."

"I'd like to think that if either of us were in that position, we'd have enough foresight to remove ourselves from the situation before it escalated to that point."

"You're telling me that you'd sit on the sidelines if it were your mother or sister out there?"

"I'm telling you that for the integrity of the investigation, I'd have to."

Mendoza laughed. "That's bullshit, and you know it."

"Of course, it's bullshit."

Pratt and Mendoza spun around at the sound of the new voice in the room. Neither of them said a word when they saw who it was.

For his part, Doctor Ice stood up from his desk and smiled, refusing to suppress the overwhelming emotion that this moment inspired in him.

"Good morning, Camille."

CHAPTER TWO

THE CONSULTANT

When the guy at the front desk clipped the visitor's badge to Camille's jacket, he smiled and asked how long she'd be staying. It wasn't an official question, just polite, everyday conversation. He undoubtedly knew of her reason for being here. He'd been briefed the same as everyone else in the building. Yet he barely blinked as she nervously approached him, choosing to greet her not with reservation, pity, or scorn, but with the warm banality that he would a regular tourist. Camille couldn't have been more appreciative of the gesture. She promptly returned his smile and replied, "Hopefully not too long."

Then she met Special Agent Stephen Wells from Crawley's B.A.U. task force, and her smile went away.

"I'm so glad you'll be joining us," he said with a solemn gaze. "I just wish it were under better personal circumstances."

Camille bit her lip and nodded as she shook his hand, sparing herself the indignity of saying something that would make this already awkward situation even worse.

"You're still thought of very highly in the B.A.U.," Wells continued. "They say the place just isn't the same without you."

Agent Wells wasn't around during Camille's tenure, and she wondered if she was staring at her replacement. "Lots of great people there."

"For sure, and they're all rooting for you."

The hush that followed only exacerbated the awkwardness.

"But enough about that," Wells finally said. "Peter and the rest of the team are waiting."

He promptly led Camille down a long corridor of dark cubicles to an open conference room where she happened upon a conversation that seemed to feature her as the main talking point.

She'd wanted to enter the room like a reasonable person and wait for the proper introductions. Instead, she was put in the uncomfortable position of defending herself.

"Of course, it's bullshit," she said in response to one of the agents and his insinuation that her presence could compromise the integrity of his investigation.

The look of abject horror on the agent's face as he turned to see her standing behind him almost made up for the sting of his insult, but not entirely.

Peter Crawley's smile was as big as Camille had ever seen it. He clearly relished the timing of her entrance. "Good morning, Camille. Please come in and join us."

She did so, glaring at the agent as she took the seat next to Crawley.

"You've already met Agent Wells from the B.A.U.," he continued. "This is Allison Mendoza and Gabriel Pratt from CBI. They're our local liaisons."

"Nice to meet you, Camille," Agent Mendoza offered with what looked like a genuine smile.

"Likewise."

Agent Pratt's greeting wasn't nearly as genuine. "I apologize if I offended you. That wasn't my intention."

"You did offend me, Agent Pratt. But in the interest of not tainting this working relationship before it begins, I accept your apology."

Pratt's jaw tightened as he turned to Crawley. "Anything else we should know, sir?"

"My briefing is finished, so I'll turn it over to Camille in case she'd like to add anything that the official report didn't cover."

"The official report is thorough enough," Camille replied curtly, refusing to feed Pratt's angst about her emotional vulnerability. In truth, the official report wasn't thorough at all. It didn't mention her anxiety about being here or the fact that she spent every minute of every day thinking about her father, or the reality that she would end the life of the person holding him without hesitation if he wasn't returned to her unharmed. But no one in this room needed to hear that, not even Peter Crawley, the man who would vouch for her until the day he died, no matter what she did. Only her father had more unconditional faith in her ability.

"Okay, since Camille doesn't have anything, let's discuss where we go from here."

"I just got off the horn with DPD admin. We're good to go on the MacPherson interview," Wells reported. "He's been slow to cooperate so far, and he's still refusing counsel, even though he was assigned a public defender two weeks ago. I honestly don't know how much we'll get out of him."

"Time isn't exactly on our side," Crawley replied as he turned a worried eye to Camille. "We'd better get something."

Crawley's expression troubled her and she looked away. Without saying a word, he'd managed to tell her everything about the current state of their investigation.

It was nowhere.

Nearly three weeks had passed since a true-crime author named Jacob Deaver confronted Camille in a quiet coffee shop, where she quietly minded her business, to pitch an idea for a biography that would detail her work as an FBI profiler; specifically, her controversial role in the apprehension of serial killer Daniel Sykes. Sykes, Deaver went on to say, was planning his own tell-all, which promised to paint Camille and her deceased partner Andrew Sheridan in the most unflattering light possible. By telling her own story in her own words, she could mitigate the damage from Sykes's book before it could ever see the light of day.

The pitch sounded reasonable, and Camille might have even considered it, were it not for the small matter of the real Jacob Deaver being reported missing one week earlier by his New York-based agent Meredith Park.

The truth, Camille would come to discover, was that the Sykes autobiography never existed, just as her biography would never exist. Daniel MacPherson, posing as Deaver, had used the cover as a means of getting close to her. For what purpose, she wasn't sure.

Then her father went missing, and the purpose became crystal-clear.

Camille sat quietly as the agents discussed the various tactics they would use to elicit MacPherson's thus far elusive cooperation. Agent Pratt seemed especially confident in his abilities.

"The problem is that the local hacks have been coming at this guy the wrong way. They're using GITMO-style tactics on him when he's nothing more than a pawn. The trick is to approach him with some understanding, make him think he's as much of a victim as anyone else."

Camille was about to roll her eyes at the suggestion, but Crawley beat her to it.

"A victim?"

"I know it sounds strange but hear me out. Daniel MacPherson is just a kid. He was angry over his sister's murder, and he wanted revenge. Sykes had already been put away, but that wasn't enough. He needed to make someone pay in a tangible way. I think we can all agree that there's another player involved, and it's that person, not Daniel, who killed those girls and abducted Deaver and Camille's father. Daniel himself admitted that he was merely a cog in the wheel. He was sad, he was pissed-off, he was desperate, and our killer exploited that. No one is saying that Daniel MacPherson is innocent. He's far from it. But if we can get him to believe that he's being used by someone who ultimately doesn't care about him, maybe he'll reconsider the lengths he's willing to go to protect that person's identity."

"You don't think that's been tried already?" Camille asked. "If you assume for a second that you can reverse psychology your way to a confession, especially from someone as calculated as Daniel MacPherson, then you don't have the first clue about what you're dealing with."

Pratt's eyes narrowed as they found Camille. "Well please enlighten me. What are we dealing with?"

Camille turned to Crawley, who gave her permission to proceed with a nearly imperceptible nod of his head.

"The person you're dealing with isn't some grieving, innocent, exploited pawn. He's deliberate, highly motivated, and very unstable. You're right that he's looking for someone to take his anger out on, and since he can't get to Sykes, I'm the next sensible target. But to think that because he didn't kill those girls he's any less dangerous than the person who did is foolish. I've been face to face with this man. I saw the way his eyes turned black with hatred when he looked at me. If he'd had the opportunity, he would've killed me the moment he saw me."

"From the sound of it, he had the opportunity. Why didn't he take it?" Agent Mendoza asked.

"Because killing me wasn't part of his plan. Not at that moment anyway. So, if he had the restraint not to kill me when he could have gotten away with it scot-free, what makes you think you can persuade him to deviate from the plan now?"

"What do you suggest then?" Crawley asked.

Camille took a deep breath. She needed steady nerves for what she was about to say. "Give Daniel exactly what he wants."

"Which is?"

"Me."

The room fell silent. All eyes were on Camille, waiting for clarification, but she suddenly felt hesitant to give it.

From the moment she agreed to join Crawley's task force – a mere two hours after her father's abduction – Camille knew what her role would be, even if no one else did.

Her visitor's badge wouldn't afford her any of the powers of an acting field agent. She wouldn't have an official firearm or shield. She couldn't arrest anyone or give orders to local law enforcement. From the Bureau's standpoint, she was here strictly as a consultant; someone with intimate knowledge of Daniel Sykes's M.O. And because the subject they were looking for was believed to be a Sykes copycat, she would presumably have intimate knowledge of his M.O. as well.

But there was only so much consulting that could occur in a case like this. Consultants talked, they pondered, they hypothesized. Camille wasn't here to hypothesize. She was here to find the person who abducted her father. And as far as she could see, there was only one way to do that.

"He wanted me here for a specific reason. Otherwise, I would be the one you all were searching for right now. I don't know what that specific reason is yet, but I don't think I'll have to wait long to find out."

"So we're just supposed to sit back and wait for you to be attacked?" Mendoza asked incredulously. "That doesn't seem reasonable."

"Especially because we have no idea who we're dealing with or what his plan is," Pratt added.

"We figure out the plan by asking," Camille said.

"You mean I'm just supposed to go in there, ask MacPherson what this plan is, and expect him to tell me?" Pratt asked.

Camille shook her head at his arrogance. "You can ask him questions until you're blue in the face, but you won't get anywhere."

Pratt smiled. "And what makes you so sure about that?"

"Because you're not me."

The smile on Pratt's face was suddenly replaced with something darker. "You're suggesting that it should be *you* who conducts the MacPherson interview?"

"That's exactly what I'm suggesting," Camille answered, her stare matching Pratt's in its intensity. "And I need to be in there alone."

"You've got to be kid—"

"Done," Crawley said, cutting off Pratt's protest. The four of us will monitor Camille and reconvene afterward to discuss. I trust that will work for everyone."

"Works for me," Agent Wells said.

Mendoza tentatively nodded her approval while Pratt quietly seethed.

"Great, then let's get to it." Crawley stood up, and the others in the room followed suit. "Camille, you can ride with me."

"Fine," she replied, keeping a wary eye on Agent Pratt as he huffed out of the conference room.

She worried that he would be a problem. Not that she didn't have solutions for blowhards like him. She'd encountered more than her share at Quantico. She just didn't have the mental stamina to deal with him right now. Most of her energy stores had already been used up, and what was left in reserve would have to be saved for Daniel MacPherson. She wondered if even that would be enough.

"You sure you're up for this?" Crawley asked with a pat on Camille's shoulder as they left the conference room.

"If I said no, would you hold it against me?"

Crawley smiled a second time. In Camille's experience, that was a record. "Not at all. As long as you don't hold it against me that I finally sweet-talked you into coming back."

Bullied would be a more apt description, but that was water under the bridge now.

"Just help me find my father, Peter."

"I will." Crawley stopped, his hand still gripping Camille's shoulder. "If it's the last thing I do."

CHAPTER THREE

ANTICIPATION

Agent Pratt was the first to enter the DPD Admin Building, followed closely by Agents Mendoza and Wells. Camille and Agent Crawley trailed behind at a considerable distance.

"You were pretty quiet in the car," Crawley said.

"What was I supposed to say?"

"You could've started by telling me how you're feeling."

"About what?"

"Confronting MacPherson. Being back in an interrogation room. Wearing that FBI shield."

"It's not a real FBI shield."

"You know what I mean."

"I'm fine."

Camille didn't need to look at Crawley to sense the doubt on his face.

"How are you really feeling?"

"I told you, I'm fine."

Crawley stopped mid-stride. "Do you remember the last time you were in this situation? The last time you conducted an interrogation?"

The image of Daniel Sykes made Camille stop too. "Of course, I do."

"It didn't turn out so fine."

She shook the memory away. "This is different."

"How?"

"Are you having second thoughts about me going in there?"

"Not at all. I'm simply looking out for you."

"I appreciate that, Peter. I really do. But I can handle myself."

"I know you can. I also know that I'm asking a lot. I just don't want it to be too much. So if it gets to be, you have to promise to tell me."

Camille looked in Crawley's eyes and saw a strain of emotion that was rarely present. He was genuinely worried about her. She hoped her brave face would be enough to allay his concern, even if it wasn't enough to conquer her own. "I promise."

Crawley exhaled quietly. "Okay. Let's go."

Upon entering the Major Crimes Division, the group was greeted by Lieutenant Owen Hitchcock and his team of detectives. Pratt, Mendoza, and Wells had already completed their round of introductions by the time Camille and Crawley caught up to them. The banter seemed friendly.

When Lieutenant Hitchcock saw Camille, he immediately broke away from the group. His arm was extended before he even reached her.

"Good to see you, Camille. I wish the circumstances were better, of course."

From what Camille could recall, she only ever saw Hitchcock under less-than-ideal circumstances. "It's good to see you too, lieutenant. Thank you for accommodating us."

"Not a problem. Your father means the world to this department. Getting him home safely is priority number one." He turned to Crawley. "I don't believe we've met. Lieutenant Owen Hitchcock."

"Special Agent Peter Crawley. Pleasure."

"Likewise."

The two exchanged a cordial handshake. Given Crawley's penchant for swinging his federal authority around like a battle ax, Camille knew the pleasantries wouldn't last.

"I take it you've already met my team." Crawley said.

"I have," Hitchcock confirmed with a smile. If he was at all leery of the group of agents and their sudden invasion of his territory, he didn't show it. "And allow me to introduce my leads, Detectives Alan Krieger and Jim Parsons. They were the first to interview MacPherson following his arrest. I'm sure you've already seen their summary, but I figured you'd want to ask them some follow up questions before you–"

"That won't be necessary," Crawley insisted. "The summary was quite thorough in explaining MacPherson's reluctance to talk. We're hoping that Camille can have more luck."

Hitchcock's smile faded. "What do you mean?"

"She's conducting the interview."

Hitchcock turned a surprised eye to Camille. "I didn't realize you were officially back with the Bureau."

"I'm not."

"Camille is here as a consultant," Crawley explained. "We believe we're dealing with a Daniel Sykes copycat, and there's no one more familiar with Sykes than Camille. She can provide valuable insight."

"She also has a deeply personal connection to one of the victims," Hitchcock said.

"I understand that."

"And you think it's a good idea to grant her access to a suspect that she's already had precarious run-ins with?"

Camille looked at Pratt and detected a hint of smug satisfaction on his face. She shot him a dirty look and turned back to Hitchcock. "That's exactly why I need to be the one in there. I'm the reason all of this is happening in the first place. I'm the one that Daniel wants, which means I'm also the one that my father's abductor wants. Your men have already tried talking to him, and they've gotten nowhere. Meanwhile, Jacob Deaver and my father are still out there, and the more time we waste in here, the harder it'll be to find them.

Camille paused to catch her breath. She knew the only chance she had to sway Hitchcock was to keep her emotions in check. "Yes, this situation is very personal, lieutenant. But I know how to conduct myself in there. I've been face to face with Daniel already. I know how he thinks. I know what his motives are. I know that he hates me. But his hatred makes him more vulnerable to emotion. And if he gets emotional, he's more likely to say something that he doesn't mean to; something that can lead us to the man we're looking for."

The tension in Hitchcock's face began to subside. "Can you assure me that things won't go sideways in there?"

"You have my word."

Hitchcock glanced back at his team. They looked less than convinced. Injured pride, Camille speculated.

"Would you at least like to have Krieger or Parsons sit in with you? They've already spent a good deal of time with him. Maybe they could offer some perspective."

Preservation of the fragile male ego was at the very bottom of Camille's priority list right now, and because of that, she responded with a simple but firm, "No."

Casting aside the terseness of her reply, Hitchcock turned to Crawley. "I hope you can appreciate just how unusual this request is. We're talking about allowing someone with no official law enforcement credentials to question the prime suspect in an ongoing criminal investigation. I don't have to tell you how that would sit with a judge should it go that far."

"No, you don't have to tell me," Crawley said. "But you know as well as I do that everything Camille has said is true."

"Again, lieutenant, it won't go sideways in there," Camille reiterated.

Hitchcock blew out a loud sigh of surrender. "Fine. But if it does, it's not my ass, or theirs." He pointed to Krieger and Parsons. "Understood?"

"Completely," Crawley replied, then turned to Camille for confirmation.

"Understood."

"Okay. If you all want to follow me, MacPherson is this way."

Hitchcock led the group down a short hallway to a monitoring station that had been outfitted with a small bank of computer monitors and several chairs. The monitors were numbered one to five. The only one currently switched on was number three. It was there that she saw him.

Clad in jailhouse orange, his hands and feet bound to a small table that Camille hoped was bolted to the floor, Daniel MacPherson looked small and feeble. But in his case, looks were deceiving. When she honed in on the grainy image of his narrow, bearded face, she noticed something else: a smile of anticipation.

He was waiting for her.

As the rest of the group situated itself inside the room, Hitchcock pulled Camille back into the hallway.

"I'm not going to lie to you, this one's got me a little nervous."

Camille tensed at his words. "Why?"

"We don't know anything about this guy aside from what you've told us. He has no criminal record to speak of, no incidents from his past that would indicate a capacity for violence, and no clear-cut motive for his involvement in Deaver's abduction. We can't get a read on him at all, and frankly, that concerns the hell out of me."

"You're looking at his motive," Camille said flatly.

"What makes you so certain?"

"He thinks I'm responsible for his sister's murder."

"Daniel Sykes is responsible for her murder."

"I didn't capture Sykes before he killed Daniel's sister and her friend. In his mind, that makes it my fault." Camille didn't want to admit that there was once a time when she believed the same thing.

"So what's his endgame? Why abduct your father and some random crime writer? Why not go after you directly?"

"That's what I need to find out. Whatever the end game is, I can certainly tell you that it's much bigger than Daniel."

"What about the murders in Pennsylvania, Missouri, and Tennessee?"

"Not him."

"How do you know?"

"I just know. Besides, there's nothing in his past that would indicate violence of that magnitude. You said so yourself."

"We could've missed something."

"He merely played his part. Someone else is orchestrating this."

"Including the murders?"

"Yes."

"Your confidence almost has me convinced."

"Almost?"

"He hasn't said five words to my detectives in over three hours of interview time. What if he decides to play the same game with you?"

"I'll make him talk to me."

Hitchcock's expression hardened. "You promised it wouldn't go sideways in there."

"It won't. Trust me."

Hitchcock blew out another loud sigh. "At this point, I don't have much of a choice, do I?" He glanced inside the monitoring room. "Can I trust your guy?"

"Agent Crawley?"

"Yes."

"For what it's worth, there's no one aside from my father who I trust more."

"So does that mean you'll go back to work for him when all of this is over?"

Camille bristled at the question but did her best to contain the irritation. "First things first, lieutenant."

Hitchcock nodded his understanding. "We'll get your dad back, Camille."

She didn't doubt the sincerity of his promise for a second, but it wasn't nearly enough to convince her. Before she could voice the thought, Crawley emerged from the monitoring room.

"Are we good to go out here?"

"I believe so," Hitchcock said before turning back to Camille. "We'll be watching closely. If you feel like it's getting out of hand in there and you need someone to come in, look into the camera and give us a nod. Okay?"

Camille knew she wouldn't need Hitchcock or anyone else to back her up, but she thought it best to humor him. "You got it."

"Okay. Good luck in there." With that, the lieutenant made his way inside the monitoring room, leaving Camille and Crawley alone in the hallway.

"You won't be giving us that nod, will you?" Crawley asked with a knowing smile.

"Of course not."

"Didn't think so. Now go in there and do that thing you do."

Camille hadn't done that 'thing' in a long time, and for the first time since agreeing to come back, she wondered if she could ever do it again. Rather than admit that to Crawley, she turned her attention to the closed door of Interview Room Three. "Something tells me Daniel is looking forward to this as much as I am. No need to keep him waiting."

THE DARKEST
POINT

A GRISHAM & SULLIVAN NOVEL

COMING SUMMER 2019

Made in the USA
Columbia, SC
16 March 2020